A Million Reasons Why

A novella

IBSN: 978-1-99-117337-9

Table of Contents

Finding people who understand and encourage us can make all the difference in achieving our goals. With that in mind, I couldn't have made it this far in my author journey without Kirsty and Anna's unwavering support and guidance.

CHAPTER ONE

ONE YEAR EARLIER - JUNE

I've often wondered how my story would end. It's one of life's only certainties. We live, we die. Everything in between is what we call life. Never once did I think it would be like this.

"How long do I have?" I ask my neurologist, Michael. He pauses, and I see a flicker of remorse flash in his eyes. We both know I'm getting worse. Today, not one of the numbers on the clock he made me draw is right. Six months ago, on the same mini-memory test, I managed to get all but two correct.

"It's hard to say—"

I raise my hand to cut him off. "Don't do that. Give it to me straight."

"You're worse than I expected," he admits with a heavy sigh. "I'd like to say five years, but there are so many variables."

I nod slowly, and my gaze drops to the floor. In the silence, I can hear the soft murmur of the city below and the soothing sound of office white noise channelling from under the closed door. Alzheimer's—I have Alzheimer's—and it means I'm going to die not knowing the letters of my own name, just as my mother did and her mother before her.

My mother was only fifty-seven when she died. A woman who'd run marathons half her life and never touched a cigarette was robbed of her dignity before life gave her a chance to comprehend the diagnosis.

Nobody in this life is immune, but seeing her struggle to remember her life and all the beautiful things in it was an unfamiliar pain. Physically, she was still alive, but inside, the jigsaw of reason had turned over, and, one by one, the pieces went missing. It started off small: from the day of the week to what she had for breakfast, and then her world started to warp. The present no longer existed, and the past became the only language her mind could speak. Day by day, she forgot everything, and then she forgot me.

The day it happened, I'd been in Glasgow for three days for a work conference and had rushed straight from the flight home to the care facility. When I arrived, she was watching *Forrest Gump* with two others in the common area.

Like always, I took a seat next to her, only this time, she didn't welcome me or give me one of her wide-eyed smiles. I'd been warned for months that the day would come, but seeing her look through me like a stranger is something no amount of pre-warning or mental preparation can arm you for.

In her confusion, I tried to explain that I was her daughter, but in her mind, I no longer existed and never had. She was gone, and now I had to grieve for her while being tortured with the replica of her left behind.

The weeks rolled into months, and she deteriorated faster than any of the specialists saw coming. She found comfort in believing I was a nurse. Some days, she called me Rosie; others, I would be Anne. Then there were times she would beg me to smother her with a pillow and others where I had to watch her cry in the realisation she'd lost the ability to control her own bowels.

I started to resent myself for allowing her to suffer, even knowing full well my hands were tied. I'd spend hours researching voluntary euthanasia and ways I could get her to

Switzerland to put an end to the misery. Unfortunately, facing the morals of thinking for her when her ability to do so had crumbled wasn't a leap I could ever take. And that is something I have never forgiven myself for.

"Have you spoken to your family yet?" Michael asks, interrupting my thoughts. He's fidgeting with his pen, unable to look at me directly.

"You and I both know I don't have any family."

He glances at me like he's seconds away from crying. At thirty-one, he is far younger than me, but over the last year, we've developed a friendship of sorts. I know about his husband and how his father-in-law hasn't yet come around to his son being gay. He's told me all about their future plans and how they are planning to have a child via a surrogate when they've both cleared their student loan debt. I know all about ethical boundaries, having been a psychologist for nearly two decades, but I allowed the friendship because I also know Michael has never had a mother figure in his life.

"I'm on my own, kid. I always have been."

"What about counselling? You need someone to talk to."

"The therapist in therapy. Now, wouldn't that be ironic?"

"I'm serious, June," he says softly, dropping his head into his hands for a moment. "This is life-changing. You're going to need support."

I know he's almost as devastated as I am about this mess, which is why I don't tell him I won't suffer. Years ago, watching my mother fight an admirable battle, I made the choice that if it came for me, I'd take matters into my own hands.

"Support for what? I've had months to prepare for this. You and I knew the odds were stacked against me. I didn't need someone then, and I certainly don't need someone now."

"You really are one of the most stubborn people I have ever met."

I roll my eyes. "Yes, I know. You've only told me that a million times before."

"Well, you are. Dare I say, I'm going to miss you."

"I'm not dead yet," I joke, which makes him flinch. "Tell me something. What should I do now? Whilst I can remember it, that is."

He places down his pen, staring at it for a moment. "Are you asking me as a friend or your doctor?"

I smile, watching him admit our relationship for what it is. "Both."

"As your doctor, I would tell you that you need to reach out to all the options of support available to you." He pauses. "As your friend, I would tell you to get on the next plane out of here. Live. Just do it while you can. Don't think. Just go."

"That sounds rather...impulsive."

He grins. "I guess now is your time to be impulsive, then."

"Alright," I say, raising my brow. "Where would you go?"

He ponders my question, and all the excitement drains from his face. "You should find him... Craig, I mean."

Jesus, did he really just say that? It's been over two decades since I last saw Craig, and now was not the time to bring him back into my life.

"Please tell me you're joking."

"You have to."

"I don't have to do anything of the sort. Of all the things I have to do before I leave this place, that most certainly isn't one of them."

I'd be lying if I said I hadn't thought of Craig every day since we divorced. We'd met in high school and dated from our senior year before we got married a week shy of my 21st birthday. Our life together was magical, and I loved him. Boy, I loved him, but sometimes, love isn't enough.

Craig wanted children; it was the one thing in life he'd always wanted. And as much as he loved me, I loved him enough to know I didn't want to be the one who prevented him from becoming a father. So, I divorced him when he was away on a month-long work trip. Labelled a cruelty by some, I knew if I brought ethics and morals into it, then he'd fight it. I didn't want or need him to fight; I needed him to accept it.

I'd limited what Michael knows. When he asked me if I was married or had children, I gave him a brief rundown of my failed marriage. Like everyone else, he asked why there hadn't been another, and it's a question I don't even know the answer to. I used to think it was the black-and-white truth that Craig and I felt unfinished. After all, there wasn't a bitter break-up where we'd argued for months and developed a hate for one another's existence. There weren't others involved or gambling on our marital vows. I'd chosen this because I loved him.

But in a number of ways, it's deeper than that because even now, two decades later, I feel the periodic pull of wanting to pick up the phone and admit I made a mistake. Only I didn't. I'd given Craig a chance to fulfil his dreams because I knew if I was his co-pilot, he'd never reach the destination. That would never be a mistake, even if I find my heart at times screaming at me it was.

CHAPTER TWO

ONE YEAR PRIOR - ABBEY

Winter has always been my favourite season since I was a little girl. There's something majestic in how even the most mundane street can become abstract with a layer of snow. Today though, I can't help but long for the warmth of a spring day. My toes are frozen, and my fingers feel dead from the knuckle down. The overnight frost has turned all the snow into ice, and our two-hundred-year-old house is struggling to reach double digits. Meanwhile, my sister-in-law, Freya, is the epitome of a walking thermos. She's due any day now, and little does she know no amount of parenting magazines or antenatal classes can prepare her for what awaits.

"How is she sleeping?"

I delay answering her. There's no nice way to say you're teetering on the edge of a psychotic breakdown and having thoughts no new mother should have.

"She's getting better," I lie, placing the kettle on the stove. "Taking it as it comes."

"I feel for you, I really do. When is Scott back?"

"Later on today."

"Well, I hope he is going to give you some much-needed rest." She slides off her chair and walks over to Aila, bobbing up and down gently in her mechanical swing. "Can I hold her?"

"Of course. Do you even need to ask?"

She shoots me a sympathetic look. "Abbey, the last thing I want to do is make your job more difficult by unsettling her."

"She's already unsettled. I somewhat doubt you could make it any worse."

"Still no answers, then?"

I shake my head again but refrain from telling her Aila gets worse with each day. She'd been an unsettled baby right from the minute she was born. First, they assumed it was colic, and then a paediatrician suspected an intolerance of sorts. Every week of her two-month life, they've run inconclusive tests and tried in vain to find an answer, but not once have we ever been within reach of a resolution.

She picks up Aila and cradles her, running the tip of her finger across her cheek, smiling. For the first time in what feels like years, Aila is calm, making soft cooing noises and fisting the neck of her jumper.

It hurts more than having seven layers of muscle torn open to have her that I no longer find enjoyment from her noises. What should fill me with love and admiration only injects me with resentment, and I find myself torn. On the one hand, I want to share my inner dark thoughts and desperation-induced mania. On the other hand, the fear of losing her outweighs any fear I have of my own feelings. Whilst, at times, I panic that all my love for her has reversed, I rest assured even on the darkest of days, there isn't a single part of me able to envision a life without her in it.

"Abbey..." She hesitates, glancing out the window. "I...I need to ask you something."

I search her face, hoping for a sign of what is coming next, but she gives nothing away.

"Are you and Scott okay?"

"Of course we are. Why do you ask?"

"This was so much easier in my head. Uh...I got this video last night."

"What kind of video?"

She places Aila down and reaches into her jacket. "It was from an unknown number, and I tried to call it, but it looks like whoever it was, disconnected the SIM shortly after sending me the video."

I wait, watching as she scrolls through her phone before handing it to me. Scott appears, and he looks drunk, sipping from a half-filled pint glass and slurring his words. "I'll get the DNA test back next week, boys, then I'll be a free man." I hear him say before I cut the video.

It wasn't the first time videos of Scott had surfaced. A month ago, Scott had gone to London for the week, and a colleague of his had reached out to me to say he was drunk in a bar, acting like a madman. They took a video and sent it to me, and even now, what he said is enough to turn the blood in my veins cold.

Swaying on his feet, he had his arm around a pretty blonde wearing a tight dress with her breasts squeezed together as he declared he was filing for divorce. Surrounded by faces who'd become our adopted family, he confessed to them how we weren't having sex and how he wished we'd never had a child. Instead of the shock and echoes of sympathy my heart longed to hear, all I heard were cheers and the clinking of glasses. Freya didn't know that. Nobody did but the person who sent me the video to begin with.

"Fre—"

She raises her hand to cut me off. "Be honest with me, Abbey. You know you can trust me, right?"

I want to believe I can, but her loyalty is to Scott, not me. "It's nothing."

"It doesn't look like nothing."

"I'm handling it."

"Are you? Because that," she says, waving her phone. "That does not look like handling it to me. He shouldn't even be drinking, Abbey."

"It isn't my place to stop him doing it!"

"You're his wife!"

"Am I? Because right now, it certainly doesn't feel like it."

She reaches for my hand, but it feels forced, like she's trying to restrain a child from touching chocolates at the checkout. "Talk to me."

"I can't," I fire back, pulling my hand from her.

Six months ago, I would have confessed everything without hesitation. She would've stopped by just as she has now, unannounced, and I'd admit how scared I am. I'd tell her how Scott and I are failing. Our marriage is crumbling, and he resents me for bringing a child into the world when it was the one thing in life he didn't want. But things are different now. They have been for a while, and I can't help but feel like she's a double agent, feeding Scott the information we no longer know how to say to one another.

"Abbey...please."

"You need to leave."

For a moment, she stares at me before Aila starts stirring in her swing. The sound of her cries floods my chest with an impenetrable warmth and fills my eyes with tears. She'd been attached to my breast every hour of the day since Scott left, and my nipples had turned to crust. Latching her was painful, and even worse was my inability to let down because of the pain. I couldn't do it anymore.

I walk over to her swing and scoop her up. By now, she's screaming, and her cheeks have flushed to a crimson red.

"Where are you going?" Freya yells as I make my way to the door.

It wasn't information she needed to know. Freya was a full believer in the way nature intended, and her house, right down to her bedsheets, was organic. If I told her I was driving to the nearest supermarket store to get my daughter a bottle and formula, she'd follow me there as if I was about to commit daylight robbery. So, I say nothing. Nothing at all.

CHAPTER THREE

SIX MONTHS PRIOR - JUNE

I am running along the Thames with a growing sense of dread. People smile and wave as they pass, and I keep on south. My turn off had to be soon. I've been running for over four miles now. I press on, my lungs burning, until I come across an empty park bench. I'm lost. After living in London for nearly two-thirds of my life, I'm lost.

I thought it was a one-off, but three days later, it happened again. I'm on my way home from the shops and find myself lost, standing in the middle of the lane, not sure whether I'm going left or right. Then, just when I think I've gathered my bearings, I realise I'm not trying to open the door to my home. I'm at someone else's house on the wrong street in a neighbourhood I don't know. It's happening, and if my mother's progression was considered quick, I was about to become a gold medallist.

"Can I help you?" I hear a voice from behind me.

I turn and see a younger gentleman no older than thirty looking at me. In his right hand are two paper bags of shopping, and in his left, he's holding his cell phone and keys.

This is his house.

"I'm sorry. I..." I pause, scanning my surroundings. There's little I can do to disguise the panic in my voice. "I don't know where I am."

He places the bags down and gives me a friendly smile. "Don't worry. I'll help you get home. Do you know where you live?"

I freeze, and it hits me—I don't remember my address. The past few weeks, I'd been using the bus and train more as roads had started to become muddled. There'd been the odd occasion where I'd taken the wrong train or confused the numbers, but I was now in uncharted territories.

"On second thought," he continues, nudging past me to open the door. "Why don't you come in for a bit?"

He's reassuring, calm, and even though we're strangers, I trust him. "Okay," I whisper, following him inside.

As a psychologist, I've seen the very best and worst of society. I learn the stranger's name is Cameron, and as he pours me a cup of tea, I know whoever his parents were, they raised him well—he's one of the best.

"What's your name?" he asks, taking a seat.

"June."

"Do you have a last name?"

I nod. "I... I think it's Brennan."

"And what year were you born?"

I freeze; I can't remember. "I...I'm sorry."

"Hey," he says softly. "Tell me something you remember from your childhood.

"It was my birthday the day Mountbatten was bombed off the Sligo coast," I say slowly. The recollection is fuzzy but it's there and I hold onto it.

"And how old were you?"

"Five... six... I know I wasn't any older than eight."

"See, now we're getting somewhere." He pulls out his phone and begins typing. "Looks like you were born on 27th August between 73-75. Once we've finished our tea, I'm going to take you to the hospital and get you seen."

Less than an hour later, Cameron drops me off at the hospital. I know he has work that evening from our limited conversation, so I encourage him to leave.

"It could be hours yet," I tell him. "There's no point in us both sitting here."

He glances over at the reception desk before bringing his eyes back to mine. "Alright, but I'm giving them my number."

"I'll be fine," I reassure. "There's no need."

"I'm going to, just in case." He stands and gathers his coat, still looking uncertain.

I'm right to make him leave as by the time a nurse leads me to a ward, the sky has descended into darkness, and the rush hour traffic I can see from the window has dwindled from a torrential river to a stream.

After a younger nurse settles me into bed, Michael and an older man appear. Michael isn't in his staple consultant attire; he's wearing a faded grey tracksuit and Nike sneakers.

"Hey, you," he says, giving me one of his customary smiles.

I give him a gentle wave. "Did I get you out of bed?"

He laughs but doesn't answer. Instead, he walks around to the right side of my bed and looks at my vitals. Suddenly, the older gentleman pipes up, "How long has your speech been affected?"

What is he talking about? My speech is fine.

"I'm...I'm not sure."

He nods and walks around to my left. "I need to run a few tests. Can you pull me towards you?" I nod, and he takes my arm into his. "Right, one, two, three."

I try my hardest, but in my eyes, I know my body is refusing to obey my simple request.

"Now, I want you to push me away. Ready? One, two, three."

He releases me gently and pats my hand. I glance at Michael, but he's head down, writing notes, and I'm not sure if he's actively avoiding me or trying to be professional.

"We'll need to keep you here for a few days," the gentleman continues. "I need to run some tests before I can be sure."

And with that, he disappears without telling me just what he is trying to be sure of.

• • • •

THE NEXT FEW DAYS, I stay at the hospital so they can run more tests, and each time they wheel me down the fluorescently lit narrow hallways, I close my eyes, praying I won't run into one of my patients or a friendly face. They pull blood from my veins, and I'm sent for two CTs of my brain, but nothing stands out. My deterioration shouldn't be this quick, and once they rule out a stroke or brain tumour, I become a medical miracle because none of it makes plausible sense.

By the fourth day, I want to leave. I want to go home, put on my work clothes and return to my office. There's too much time to think confined within the four walls, and in the silence, I realise how alone I truly am.

Another day passes, and Michael informs me they want to run some tests on my heart. In his words, even though it doesn't appear to be a stroke, sometimes there's other things which could point to it being one. Later that afternoon, as I expected, the results have done nothing other than confirm my Alzheimer's was on its own self-driven rampage.

"It might be time to consider moving to an assisted living facility," one of the doctors suggests, handing me my discharge papers.

Michael wasn't here as he was on his day off. Had he been, I would've thrown something at him.

"Excuse me?"

"This disease is progressive."

"Tell me you didn't just suggest I move somewhere to waste away till I die."

"That isn't what the facilities are—"

"Quit it with the shite now. It's exactly what they are. You and I both know it's nothing more than a holding cell until your number is called."

"They'll help you manage."

I shake my head and shove the discharge papers into my bag. "I'll manage...on my own."

"Ms Brennan, I strongly suggest—"

"I strongly suggest you leave before I file a complaint."

A flash of hurt crosses his face, and I realise I'm acting too flippant.

"Look," I say, searching for his name tag. "I know you mean well, Andrew, but you aren't my normal doctor. Let's leave the suggestions to him."

"It was actually Michael that suggested it."

Of course it was. Although he was kind and saw beauty in everyone's multi-dimensional shades, Michael was born with the shortest backbone imaginable.

"While I appreciate your concern, I'm more than capable of handling myself."

"Can I... Can I at least give you a brochure? Then you know your options."

I shake my head and zip the bag shut, but he asks again.

"Fine," I say, grabbing it from his hand and stuffing it into the side pocket. "Feel better now?"

He shoots me a sympathetic look. "I guess."

CHAPTER FOUR

PRESENT - ABBEY

Lola is a woman who reminds me of my favourite pair of Teddy Edward jeans. Her advice no longer fits, and the need for her has dwindled into a questionable existence. Still, I can't seem to let her go. Maybe it's loneliness that sees no harm in our sessions where we discuss everything but my endless problems. Or maybe the answer is simpler than that. After all, Lola, with her peroxide blonde and sixties-inspired hair right down to her ridiculous flamboyant clothing, is the only person in the world who no longer scares me.

"You know," she says, staring across at me as she's cataloguing my every thought. "How would you feel about visiting the site?"

My stomach suddenly flips. "The site?"

"It's the one thing left on my list for you to do." She leans forward and picks up a piece of paper, flashing it to me.

A hot flush surges through me, flooding my skin with an uncomfortable warmth. I try to hide it, but from Lola's raised brow to the inquisitive widening of her eyes, I know she sees my discomfort. "I...I don't think that's a good idea."

"I do. For starters, it would mean you aren't adding an extra ten miles onto your journey just to go to work. And truthfully, I am running out of ideas on how we move forward. I think you're ready."

"Well, I don't," I stammer.

"Abbey..."

"Lola, no. I'm not ready. I'm sorry."

For a moment, we sit in silence. In the distance, we can hear the soft murmur of voices in the room next to us and the monotonous white noise of the city below. Suddenly, Lola leans forward and grabs a card.

"I think we've reached the end of our journey, Abbey. For the last two months, we've spent our weekly hour in idle chit-chat. I'm wasting your time and money letting this continue."

Every inch of me wants to break into tears, but holding them on a leash is the reality. Truth is, I've been waiting for this day for weeks. Lola is one of the most in-demand therapists in the city, and the hours she wastes with me could be best reserved for someone who actually needs it. Not a twenty-five-year-old me who needs friends instead of a fifty-quid-an-hour therapist.

"This guy here, he is amazing. Should you need assistance in the future, that is." She pauses and looks down at the card. The way she stares at it, running her thumb over its edge, and the hesitation in her voice makes me know the feeling isn't one-sided. We'd become friends, even if it was ethically wrong.

"Abbey, I give you my word, he may come across as arrogant at first, but he's the best. I'll even let you in on a little secret: he's my therapist, too."

"Your therapist?" I question, trying to remove the sadness from my voice.

She laughs and passes me the card. "Even therapists need therapy."

We both stand and hug each other. It isn't one of those polite hugs shared between strangers. No, we hug each other like two sisters in an airport where one's taking a one-way ticket into the unknown, and the other's life is staying the same. And maybe that is one of life's cruelties. Sometimes, those we meet in life are only there for a fleeting moment. Yet, their purpose and effect have profound impacts on who we are and, perhaps, more importantly, the eventual person we'll become.

By the time five o'clock hits, my eyes are burning from scouring the web on the latest fad, and I'm tethering the edge of a psychotic, hunger-induced breakdown. With only half an article left to do, I press on, word by word, until I'm enveloped by darkness. With my stomach raging and the torrential downpour outside still beating down, I make my way home. I keep my head low, trying to avoid prying eyes from the gridlocked traffic surrounding me and find myself reflecting on Lola's words. If I was to walk past where it happened, I'd be home in less than twenty. Taking my usual route is forty minutes on a good day. My steps slow as I reach the corner, and I take a deep breath. It's a choice of left or right, but in the moment, it feels like life and death.

Would Lola, a woman whose judgement I'd come to trust more than my own, really suggest such a thing if it would derail me? I'd been avoiding it, hoping one day I wouldn't fear it so much. It isn't so much the concept of their final resting place or the revision of that day which scares me. It's me. I caused the accident. I know I did. No matter how much Lola and every other person who considered their word gospel on the matter says otherwise.

The sound of a car's horn beeps in the distance, pulling me from my thoughts, and I glance to the right. It's a road I once drove most days, and as I watch a taxi disappear into the distance, it feels shrouded in mystery.

"You can do this," I whisper to myself.

I take a deep breath and start walking. It almost stirs an unnatural unease in my legs. For so long, they'd become accustomed to the same, customary long-winding road that takes twice the time. I walk for a further five minutes with my head down, and when I look up again, I see it. To others, it's just a road. To me, it's a polaroid of all I've lost.

For a while, I stare at it, watching the world give it little regard. It's a bittersweet truth we all come face to face with at one point in our lives. What feels and is rightfully significant to us, often is nothing more than a flick of paint splatter on a much larger painting.

I stop and close my eyes. For a moment, the world around me drowns out, and my breathing steadies. In an instant, I feel it. I feel the way my body jolted. I hear the sound of glass breaking and metal scrunching like notebook paper. Then there's silence, and I wait, listening to hear a soft murmur of her breath or a faint cry, but there is nothing. Nothing at all.

When I open my eyes again, I know I can't go any further. Not today, at least. So, I turn around and am about to head back the way I came when I come across a woman dressed in a fluorescent yellow rain jacket and knee-high Wellingtons. I'm not sure what makes me look twice, but there is something in her demeanour that sets off all my dormant maternal instincts.

She paces for a second, turning around in a half-circle before walking to the overpass railing. I'm about to look away when I see her hook her leg into the bottom ledge, and it hits me—she's going to jump.

"Oi," I scream, dropping my umbrella. It must have been less than fifteen seconds from the moment I saw her before I tackled her to the ground. She lets out a humph as I'm lying on top of her.

"What the hell were you thinking?" I say, pushing myself off her. I expect to see a teenager or, at best, a woman the same age as me, so I'm in pure shock when I realise the person I've pinned to the ground is a woman who looks in her early forties.

"I'm sorry," she says. She takes a moment to gather herself, and I help her to a stand. After wiping the hair glued to her cheek away, I get a closer look of her face. She could pass as a younger Julie Christie look-alike with the same piercing eyes and perfectly proportioned lips. For a while, we stare at each other, neither one of us breaking the gaze. Her eyes are intense, focused on mine as if I am the only other person in the world, and I see it firsthand—fear, sadness, and the translucent pain encased inside.

"I...I wasn't going to jump," she finally says, looking away.

"Yes, you were."

"You're right. I was."

"What's your name?"

"June." She stiffens and folds her arms.

"Like the month?"

She nods."And the second wife of Johnny Cash."

I smile, but she doesn't flinch. "I like it."

"Yours?"

"Abbey."

I catch her eyes again, and she doesn't look away. They appear softer now, laced with a hint of memory she doesn't want to revisit.

"Short for Abigail?"

I shake my head. "Nope. Just Abbey."

"I knew an Abbey once. It's not a common name on its own."

"No, it's not. Guess I can blame my father for that one," I say, reaching into my pocket. I pull out my phone to call the police, but before I can stop her, June swipes it from my hands.

"What are you doing?"

"No cops. Please. I promise I'm okay."

"Okay," I say, raising my hands for a split second. I'm not sure if I believe her, but the choice to consider otherwise now feels irrelevant. "Can I have my phone back?"

She nods and passes it back to me.

"Do you want to go somewhere and talk?"

"Talk?"

"Talk about what's bothering you and why you thought jumping off a bridge into rush hour traffic was a good idea."

"I wasn't thinking. There's your answer." She smooths her hair, glancing at the on-coming traffic.

"I can tell. But right now, since you won't let me ring the cops, I can't let you out of my sight."

"Because?"

"Because I can't trust you to make good choices, for starters."

She glances down the street. "How old are you, Abbey? Twenty?"

"Twenty-five. Why?"

June straightens her jacket. "It figures."

"Excuse me?"

"You younger generation want to fix the world. Thing is, you can't. The world is and forever will be broken."

She starts walking, and I follow her. The rain has started falling so heavily I can barely make out her silhouette in the deluge as it starts weaving its way down the hill.

"The only thing broken about the world is that it's full of broken people," I yell, chasing after her.

She laughs and quickens her pace.

"Where are you going?"

"Do you always ask so many questions?"

I quicken my pace to match hers. "When I'm worried about someone, yes."

"Why do you care? You don't even know me."

"And what if I wanted to?" I say the first thing that comes to mind, and when it comes out, I realise how ridiculous it sounds when she stops in her tracks and gives me one of those infamously formidable 'you didn't just say *that*' glares.

"You want to know me?"

"Well, I want to know why you thought that was your only option," I say, gesturing behind us.

CHAPTER FIVE

PRESENT - JUNE

Listening to the rain beat down like an off-beat drum, I take a seat, watching the world go by. I've started to forget the days of the week, even though I read the paper every morning, and I've lost over a stone. Last night, I was up till the early hours researching the forums of Dignitas, and all it did was fill me with sadness.

Nobody would be beside my bed, watching me take my last breath. There'd be no funeral or gathering celebrating my life's work or the impact my presence had on others. I'm on my own, and while that had never bothered me in the past, now, it haunts me.

A couple crosses the road huddled under an umbrella, and my thoughts drift to Craig. He should be here with me, navigating the turbulent waters I've found myself in. And now, I don't even know where he is in the world. Rumours circled he'd moved north and taken a teaching position in a remote village on the Isle of Skye, but others say he moved to Wales. Wherever he is, I only hope he found happiness.

I reach across for my phone and search for him once again. It's been months since I last looked, and he pops up with twelve mutual friends, smiling with his arms around a pretty brunette. He hasn't aged like I have. His face still has a softness to it, and even through a screen, it fills me with nostalgic comfort. I shift my focus to the woman. She carries a familial resemblance, reminding me of his late mother in a way from her porcelain skin and the auburn hair that shapes their similar heart-shaped face.

Then it hits me; it isn't his wife. It's his sister.

I click on the photo, and sure enough, she's tagged. He'd kept his previous photos with her private, but this one is public, and I'm able to click on her profile to confirm it.

When we met, his sister, ten years younger than him, had been doing an exchange student experience in Italy. She fell in love, and I'd only met her on a handful of occasions, so it made sense why I didn't recognise her. All these years, I'd thought he'd forged a new life with someone else. What if, like me, he spent his years surrounded by the ghosts of the past?

Placing my phone flat down beside me, I start crying. I'm not even sure why it upsets me to consider that I might've got it wrong.

Suddenly, I jolt as my phone rings. It's Courtney. The NHS employed her as my junior when I told them of my diagnosis, and with two weeks left until I retire, she's started to shadow me more. At first, it was fine, but when you've worked on your own for so long without restriction or anyone to answer to, solitude becomes a preferred currency.

"Courtney," I say, wiping my face. "How can I help?"

"Did you forget we had an appointment this morning?" Wherever she is, it's noisy, and I can barely hear her.

"I don't work on a Thursday."

"June...it's...it's Wednesday."

"No, it's not." I stand and walk over to the calendar pinned to the fridge. In the background, I hear a door shut, and it becomes eerily quiet. "Today is Wednesday the 14th," I say, noting the one diagonal line.

"Are...are you feeling okay?"

"Why are you acting funny?"

"It's not the 14th, June. It's...Well...it's—"

"God dammit, not you, too. Just say it!"

"It's not the 14th...June, it's...it's the 20th."

"No...it..." I pause and stare at the calendar, unable to process what she's telling me. Instead of marking the calendar in descending order, it's backwards, and I've missed an entire week in between. "I'll be there in thirty," I tell her and quickly hang up before she presses me with more questions.

I arrive at the office less than an hour later, and Courtney is still with one of our regulars when I do. After making myself a coffee, I head into my office and take a seat to wait. It doesn't take long, and within ten minutes, Courtney comes barrelling in wearing one of the concerned masks I've seen far too many times before. I'd refrained from telling her about the Alzheimer's diagnosis because I didn't want or need her sympathy. If she was going to learn from me and learn well, she didn't need to be distracted by something neither of us could do anything about.

"Take a seat," I say, gesturing to the paired seats in front of my desk. "We need to talk."

How do you tell someone you're losing your mind? I've asked myself this question more than once over the years as individuals from all walks of life contend with the same notion. It's one thing to lose your mind, and then there's actually knowing you are but are powerless to prevent it.

"I have Alzheimer's," I say. "It's...well, I guess you could say it is advancing faster than anyone expected—myself included."

She looks me up and down, and her face folds into a soft scowl. "What are you talking about?"

I say it again, only this time as the last word falls out of me, we share a silent exchange confirming it.

"You're too young." Her voice reduces to a whisper. "I don't understand."

"Neither do I. One of those unfortunate things, I guess."

"Surely there has to be something they can do."

"Other than meds, which give me round-the-clock nausea and the worst diarrhoea imaginable, unfortunately not."

"So, this is why you're leaving?"

I nod. "There's more. I don't think it's safe for me to continue for another two weeks. Courtney...I...I'm losing my sense of time. I read things a half dozen times and have little recollection of it. I barely have any faith in my functioning, let alone to be advising others on how to restore their own. And then I worry I'm putting clients at risk because three decades of learning and experience are crumbling beneath my fingertips. If it wasn't for me needing to ensure that you have all the skills you need to continue on here, I would've left a long time ago." I pause. It's hard for me to admit defeat and even harder for me to accept that my time as a psychologist is done. I've dedicated years to helping others; in a way, it'd become the identity of who I am. Without it, the me I know doesn't exist. "Thing is, you're more than capable, Courtney. You always have been."

Mid-afternoon rolls around, and I organise an urgent Skype call with the head office and tell them it's time for me to go. As I expected, I'm met with generic acknowledgements of my service and how I'll be missed. They ask if I'm sure, and once I convince them I am, they press me on Courtney's performance.

I don't have to lie. Courtney's fierce, not easily manipulated, and still manages to give empathy where needed while keeping her feelings at bay. In a few years time, I have no doubt she's going to be a great psychologist, if not one of the best. I relay this to them, and the conversation draws to a close.

"Are you going to be okay?" Lou, one of the senior clinicians, asks.

I scan the pixelated faces and force a smile. "I have to be."

The rest of the afternoon becomes a haze of packing belongings and sending customised farewell emails to my patients. Courtney and I don't talk about it. Our relationship had always been somewhat precarious. We weren't friends. At times, I questioned if we even liked each other, but deep within all the multi-faceted layers of our interactions, we respected one another.

"You know," she says, watching me box the last of my textbooks. "Dare I say I'll kind of miss you."

I look across at her and see she's trying to wrangle in her emotions. "Don't get sentimental now."

"I'm serious. For what it's worth, I always admired you. The way you understand people, it's a gift."

"I'll have to come back for this tomorrow. I walked today, and it's bucketing outside."

"Of course," she says, her eyes trailing over to the ominous darkening sky outside. "You sure you don't want a ride?"

"I think today, of all days, I need to walk."

Something changes in my demeanour as I slide on my Wellingtons and head outside. Over the years, I've read several studies on how the weather can interfere with our moods, but it isn't rain or the cool February air dragging me under; it's my reality.

I'm losing. The water is rising fast, my days are numbered, and everything around me has changed and become a key to a life I no longer own. My reflection is becoming stranger by the day, and I fear all I am is dissolving before my eyes.

As I dredge up the puddled footpath on the bridge, past a dozen grid-locked cars and pedestrians, the world fades into silence. I'm aware of my heart beating and the air around each breath condensing into a fog, but there's nothing else. Just me, alone with my thoughts, growing louder by the second, whispering to me something I never dreamt imaginable.

Jump.

If you work in mental health long enough, you'll find suicide is more often than not an impulsive act. It's a need, a longing to escape a pain that feels unfathomable to contend with. There's no room for the aftermath and certainly no comprehension of the lifelong scars it can etch into another. In the moment, tunnel-visioned and afraid, nothing other than escape matters.

I hook my leg into the bottom rail of the overpass, watching the traffic below me as it moves like red and yellow confetti in a free-flowing stream. It'd be instantaneous; anyone with half a brain would know that. I'd be here one minute and gone the next. The idea seems comforting and a way to escape all my feelings of failure and hopelessness, yet something pulls me back. What if it causes an accident? What if I land on someone and give them a life sentence they never asked for?

And then the biggest fear of all, what if this becomes what I am remembered for and not the woman I once was?

Before another hesitant thought can surge to the surface, I hear a woman's voice from behind me, and I'm flung to the ground.

"What the hell were you thinking?" she yells, and I lie there with rain seeping into my eyes, unable to give her an honest answer.

CHAPTER SIX

PRESENT - ABBEY

I hail a taxi, and we make our way down to Camden. Neither of us speaks until the taxi, unable to park, drops us on the corner of a busy intersection.

"Where is this place?" June asks as we start walking.

"Just a little further," I say. "Up there, at the end."

"It's kind of out of the way, isn't it? Couldn't we have just gone to the Tavern?"

I shake my head. The last time I'd gone to the Tavern, I'd been followed home by a man who thought he was a real-life Jack Sparrow who could swoon women with his accent and liquor-tainted breath.

"It's kind of a local secret," I say. "They do the best Italian food here."

A minute passes, and I slow my steps. I hadn't been here since Scott and I were together, yet, the place hasn't aged a day. A few dozen cars were parked in front as they always were, and the walls were still lined with the historic Victorian brick facade. For peak hour, it's oddly quiet, and after sliding off our coats, we take a seat at a booth across from one another.

"So,' I say, reaching for a menu. "Where do you work?"

"If you must know, I was a psychologist. And...well, today was my last day." June sits back, the heavy, discerning quality of her gaze sending a prickling down my backbone. It feels like she's looking right through me, past the shiny politeness to the jagged edges underneath.

"Did you retire?"

"I guess you could say that."

I nod, trying to come up with what to say next. "Will you miss it?"

An irritable laugh escapes her lips. "Is this really why you brought me here? To exchange small talk and pretend we're friends?"

"Are you always this rude?"

"Do you always invite strangers out for dinner?"

I scowl, lowering my voice. "Do I need to remind you what you were about to do yourself?"

"Actually, you don't know for certain I would've, and neither do I. Was I considering it? Yes. If I *was* actually going to go through with it is something neither of us will ever know."

Just then, the server approaches our table. "Can I get you two anything while you're looking at the menu? A drink, perhaps?" she asks sweetly.

"Two shots of tequila and a double shot of whisky. Jameson if you've got it," June says without looking at either of us.

"And for you, ma'am?"

"I'll have the same," I say, glaring at June. It's been one hell of a day, and I'm trapped here with a woman who happens to be the most challenging person I've ever met.

June raises her brow as she watches the server disappear with our order.

"You're not the only one who's had a bad day," I say under my breath, reaching across for a menu.

"Well, then," she replies. "Just as well tequila fixes everything."

Our drinks arrive a short while later, and we settle into easy conversation, uninterrupted even when our order is brought to us. I'm not sure if it's the alcohol or whether somewhere in the space of thirty minutes we'd developed an understanding and mutual respect for one another, but it's nice.

We talk about life, and I tell her how I was hoping to resign from my copywriting job before the year's end to travel. She seems fascinated by this, asking lots of questions as to where I'd go, and then she asks about Scott. It's a simple question, asking who I'm taking with me, and yet giving her an honest answer feels like the words could choke me.

"Actually, I don't have a partner. I did, but he died." I pause, trying to gauge her reaction. She gives nothing away, her eyes continuing to pierce me with a fixed stoic stare. "It's been nearly a year, and I can't even think about being with someone else. Tell me that's normal. Better yet, tell me how to get over him."

"I don't give advice," she says, bluntly.

"But you're a psychologist?"

"Exactly. And I'm not any more. Besides, psychologists don't give personal advice. We listen, educate, and help you make your own decisions, but at the end of the day, only you know what's best for you and how you feel." She raises her hand to get another drink. "What I can tell you is this: for some people, grief, whether it's death or mourning the end of a relationship, can sometimes be a life-long void. I've seen women bed another within days and those who find everlasting love weeks after the loss. You know what else I've seen? Those who have lost the key to their life's existence and never recover the ability to unlock what feels like home again. Neither is right or wrong, but Abbey, you're young. Give it time. You might find an Italian stallion in the Riviera or an equally delightful monsieur in France to have a bit of craic with."

I laugh. “I doubt that.”

“If you don’t mind me asking, what happened?” Her face softens, and in an instant, June went from someone who was nothing more than a stranger to someone I felt I’d known my whole life.

“I was in an accident...a car accident. We had a little girl, Aila. She was nearly two months old at the time, and they both died in the crash. And it’s crazy, I feel so stupid and weak because he was a complete bellend to me towards the end. He resented me for having Aila when he wanted me to consider other options. I thought he was just scared. His home life... It hadn't been easy and I thought it would help him to heal the inner child and all of that. We’d always been such a team, I never thought having a child would be the thing to tear us apart but it did. Somehow as awful as it was, I love him...I still love him, and at the same time, I’m so angry. I’d diagnose myself as depressed because, on the one hand, I hate life without him, but on the other, I’m so grateful to be here when I could’ve died.

“And where does your daughter fit in? Do you hate life without her?”

“Of course I do, but she’s gone.”

“So is Scott?”

I shake my head. “You know what, forget it.”

“Hang on now. You’re holding onto something. I can see it clear as day; I’m trying to figure out if it’s him or her. Here’s another question for you. Do you miss him or do you miss the version of him you’re choosing to remember?”

“What do you mean?”

"Our processing of grief can rewrite our memories—" Suddenly, she pauses, scanning the restaurant with a look of confusion.

"Are you okay?"

She doesn't answer me and pats the side of her cheek like she's trying to awaken from an afternoon siesta.

"June?"

Her eyes come back to me. "I'm sorry...do I know you?"

"Uh...not exactly. We met an hour ago."

"We did?"

I nod, reaching into my jacket for my phone. "Can I get you something? Water?"

She shakes her head and reaches into her bag, pulling out a notebook. The pages are all highlighted in a colour-coded system, and there's an insert containing a list of numbers.

"Okay, today is Monday," she whispers to herself before reaching for her phone to check the time. "It's just gone seven in the evening, and I am in a restaurant—"

"It's Wednesday," I interrupt, confused. "You walked here with me after we met...on the overpass." I refrain from telling her why we met and hope with a little prompt, she'd be able to connect the dots, but all it does is add to the confusion.

"I'm sorry, I know I should know who you are, but right now, you're a stranger." She keeps her head low for a moment before lifting her eyes to mine. "I...I have alzheimer's."

I feel a spark of relief surge through me because it suddenly makes sense. The change in June—the sudden confusion, abrasiveness, and hostility—it all makes sense.

CHAPTER SEVEN

PRESENT - JUNE

Staring out the window, the taxi pulls away, and I feel like I'm dreaming. It has started to snow, coating everything in a fine layer of dust, and neither Abbey nor I say a word to one another as we start weaving through the streets. After a while, I bring my eyes back to her; she's scrolling her phone with a look of concern. Her lips are pursed, and she keeps her eyes intently focused on the screen. Finally, we pull into my street and disembark.

"I'm coming in," she says authoritatively, watching as the taxi disappears into the distance.

I agree, not because I want to but because of the way she phrases it makes me feel like it'd be impossible to say no.

Once inside, she gets to work. First, getting the boiler running and then putting the kettle on. There's no awkwardness. She walks around as if each of the four walls was her own before finally taking a seat opposite me in the living room.

"You must have a family I can call." She keeps her tone measured and calm, but I sense there's an element of disbelief weaving its way in.

"Believe me; there's not."

"I can't just leave you here."

"Actually, yes, you can. We didn't even know each other five hours ago."

She stands and ignores my remark. "You must have someone. What about a friend? Partner?"

I study her for a moment, unsure of what or how much to tell her. She's different in a way I can't pinpoint. Buried under all her sadness, the weight of regretful decisions, and remorse, I'm not sure if she reminds me of a younger version of myself or the complete opposite. In the end, I keep it brief.

"I was married once. Maybe I'm one of those people that is never able to find themselves again after it happened. Craig, he was my life, and when we split up, all those I thought were my friends picked his side. I guess you could say it scarred me. Even with all my years dealing with trauma and the complex ways we deal with it, I couldn't handle my own. It made me a recluse, scared of the outside world and even more scared of becoming attached to those in it. So, no; there's no friends and certainly no partner."

For a moment, Abbey seems to disappear into herself before she walks over to the wall and studies the row of photographs hanging in a near-perfect straight line. I'd kept most of the ones of Craig boxed and only kept one, the photo of us on my graduation day, out for display. I watch as she studies it, the room falling into silence. Finally, she asks the question I already sensed she'd ask. "What happened to you and him? Did you just grow apart?"

I hate the questions because although time had continued with little regard, a part of me wasn't ready to face it. "I guess you could say that. He wanted children. I didn't."

The room falls silent, and I glance out the window, watching each flake of snow barricade the windows one by one. Winter had always been his favourite, and as another flake falls, obscuring the road from view, my thoughts drift to him and the last conversation we had about children.

It was a week before Christmas, and I'd arrived home from work to find he'd discovered my hidden stash of birth control. After learning I carried the APOE-e4 gene, I'd been secretly taking the pill because part of me didn't know how to tell him, and the other part believed if I did, he'd leave. He eyed me like prey as I walked in the door, seated at the dinner table with a half-drunk bottle of Johnny Walker and the scrunched cardboard packet emptied before him.

"What the fuck is this, June?" he yelled once the door was closed.

I closed my eyes, swallowing hard. In his voice, I could feel his pain. I'd lied to him, and as he demanded I answer him, his words breaking and trembling, I felt the wound of betrayal split my chest in half. If I'd been honest, he'd tell me it was a fifty-fifty chance. One way or another, he'd rationalise that the risk of giving our child the gene didn't outweigh the possibility that his genes would be stronger. And maybe a part of him didn't care. He'd argue that a chance at fifty good years is better than no life at all when my maternal instincts would counter how every child born into this life should have a chance to live a full life, not just three-quarters of one.

"How could you?"

I couldn't look at him, my eyes filling with tears.

"Five years, June. We've been trying for five years."

In all our years together, he'd never laid a finger on me, but as he pressed me against the wall, his breath smelling like acidic caramel and charred oak, I knew he wanted to hurt me—not for who I was, but for the choice I'd made and the web of lies spun as a consequence.

"I know. I'm sorry."

"You're sorry?" He rests his head against mine, holding my jaw with his left hand. "Is that it?"

"I don't know what you want me to say."

"How about why? Let's start there!"

"Craig...I..."

"Why? I don't understand." He sounded defeated like I'd wounded him in a way nothing else could. Finally, he let me go, shaking his head with the muscle of his jaw pulsing. "Did you ever want them or was that a lie, too?"

"Of course I did."

"Then what changed?"

"Me," I whispered, the tears falling hard and fast. "I changed."

I've rehearsed the scenario in my head a thousand times, but as the sound of a phone ringing fills the air, pulling me away from replaying the montage, I know today won't be another.

"It's yours," Abbey says, pointing to my bag.

I lean forward and pull it into my lap. It's Michael; I know from the hideous ringtone he'd given himself weeks ago.

"I thought our time was up," I say, watching as Abbey uses the diversion to head back into the kitchen.

"Well, now you aren't my patient, can I not simply call a friend?"

"You'll get yourself in trouble."

"I won't tell if you don't. Now, tell me, how are you?"

I glance over at Abbey who by now is opening cupboards with a muddled expression and lower my voice. "Today wasn't good."

"Do you want to talk about it?"

"Not overly."

"Have you eaten today?"

I laugh. "What is this? Twenty-one questions?"

In the background, I hear Michael's partner start singing an off-tune rendition of "Bohemian Rhapsody" loudly. "I'm just checking in. You worry me."

"If you worry about all your patients like this, you'll end up in an early grave. Go. It's the weekend and the last thing you need to be doing is concerning yourself with the likes of me."

He hesitates, and in it, I sense I've gotten the day of the week wrong again.

"You're still keeping your diary, aren't you?"

"Yes," I say. "Now go."

He hangs up and Abbey comes back and appears annoyed. "You have no food in your cupboards."

"I'm well aware of that," I say, placing my phone down.

"I'll be back soon." She walks over to the coat rack and slides on her coat.

"Where are you going?"

She doesn't answer me and pats her pocket.

"Abbey..."

Before I can stop her, she heads out the door.

CHAPTER EIGHT

PRESENT - ABBEY

"What are you doing out this late?"

I turn to see Levi in the aisle. He's dressed in his staple Pink Floyd oversized tee and Doc Martens, which for the life of me, I can't work out why, well past his emo days, he still dresses like a teenager.

He joined our company back last summer, and everyone in the office had tried to set us up since. And while he has the looks, passing for a younger Lenny Kravitz with his olive skin and eyes that could seduce even the most loyal of women, he's a walking red flag.

At thirty-two, word on the street is Levi hasn't had a relationship longer than a few months. He still lives with his grandparents and drives a car he can't afford. If I wanted to become workplace gossip and give my self-confidence a superficial inflation, I'd take that ride home. Better yet, I'd ask him if he wants dinner and take him back to mine. But there is one thing wrong with that picture: I haven't slept with anyone but Scott, and even though there is a part of me who misses sex, the other part of me finds comfort knowing there's a part of me only he has.

"I could ask you the same thing," I say, putting a packet of shortbread into the trolley. Without knowing what June eats, I've resorted to a guessing game, hoping like Cinderella, the shoe fits.

He reaches over me and pulls down a double packet of chocolate-covered digestives. "I'm shopping for my nan. She can't drive, and my parents are away."

"Me, too," I lie.

"You're shopping for your nan?"

I stare into my trolley for a second, and my eyes catch on some bladder control pads I'm not sure June uses. "Yeah...she's uh...she's not well...Alzheimer's."

"Ah, damn. I'm so sorry. Do you want a ride back?"

"I'm okay tonight. I'll walk."

"You know it's coming down out there now?"

I glance out the window and see full-on the snow has turned into a full-on blizzard and sigh. "Ugh, you've got to be kidding me."

"I can give you a ride; don't stress. I only live around the corner from you."

I try to hide my discomfort. How does Levi even know that? He's either checked my employee file or Kat from accounts has been feeding him information. My bet is on the latter since she's been the most dominant in the *live a little* crusade for months.

"Thanks for the offer, but it's alright."

He doesn't buy it. I can tell from his confused expression. "Have I made you uncomfortable? It feels like you're trying to dodge me."

Suddenly, I lose all control over what happened.

"I'm not shopping for my nan," I blurt out. "There was this woman on the bridge...she was going to jump, and then I saw what was happening, and I...and I tackled her to the ground. Then I suggested we go out for dinner, and she...she got confused while we were out, and now, I'm buying her groceries because she lives on her own, and there was no food in the cupboard and...and I can't leave her there, Levi, knowing she has no food in her house and nobody checking in her."

He gapes at me; I gape back.

"She has Alzheimer's and no family, and I'm worried what she will do when I leave!" His confusion deepens, and I continue. "I just...I'm not avoiding you. There's just a lot...I mean a lot going on right now."

His eyebrows furrow. "Slow down a minute. You said she was going to jump as in...suicide?"

"Yes."

"And you didn't call the cops?"

"No...she didn't want the police involved. I...I think I can help her."

He glances toward the checkouts and then meets my eyes again. "You're not a psychologist, Abbey; you do realise that?"

"Of course, I know that. June...she doesn't need a psychologist."

"And you know that because?"

"Because right now, she needs a friend."

"I've no idea what to say to you right now." He studies me, and I can't work out whether he is impressed or that I've verified the lonely and socially awkward rumours Kat seems to love spreading.

"She needs someone to help her!"

"I can see that."

"It sounds crazy. I know you're thinking that, but—"

"I'm not thinking that," he interjects. "To be honest, part of me is trying to wrap my head around what you just said."

I sigh, reaching for a packet of digestives. "While you catch up, can you at least tell me what to feed her?"

His eyes glance at the trolley, and he lets out a short laugh. "I can help with that."

For the next thirty minutes, Levi, aisle by aisle, helps me create a food itinerary which should last June at least a fortnight. He doesn't ask questions, though I sense there are a million inside he wants to ask but doesn't know how. We go through the same checkout after one another, and I put the order, twice my weekly salary onto my credit card before we slowly walk in unison to the automated exit doors.

"Are you going to walk with all of that?" Levi asks, slowing his steps. He reaches into the left pocket of his jacket and pulls out his keys. "My offer of a ride still stands."

"Okay," I say slowly. "On one condition. You can't tell anyone about this and no police. This woman, she trusts me."

He hesitates, and in his eyes, I see the moral conflict take hold. Finally, he nods. "Deal."

We drop off his nan's groceries first. She lives less than a mile away from June in a semi-detached that smells of peppermint lollies and cigarettes. Like Levi, she's gorgeous. Her skin, unlike June's, which looks like she'd spent half her life under the sun, is unblemished. Even her wrinkles appear soft as if her face was butter and time had used a blunt knife to etch age lines in uniform places. By the time we leave, it's nearing midnight, and I worry June will question if I really am coming back. I don't have her number to call, and as Levi and I scour the street, it takes me three attempts to identify her flat under the thick blanket of snow.

"June," I say, opening the front door. She doesn't answer me, but from the living room, I can hear deep breathing amplified by the surrounding silence. Levi helps me bring in all the groceries and offers to help me unpack.

"I'm okay," I say, glancing across at June fast asleep. "It's late. You go."

Levi's eyes trail mine. "What will you do?"

"I haven't thought that far ahead."

"She's a stranger."

He's right, and in theory, she is. But however unexplainable to some, it doesn't feel that way.

"I think I'll stay here tonight. Just to be safe."

"Please tell me you're joking."

I shoot him a look. "What if she goes straight back to the bridge when she wakes up?"

"If she does, it really isn't your problem."

"I'm not leaving her."

He reaches across me and picks up a tin of beans. "If you stay, so will I."

"Absolutely not."

"What if she wakes up and freaks out that you're here? Did you think that far ahead?"

"I guess not," I admit.

"Tomorrow, we'll hatch a plan."

"We?"

"I'm involved now."

I hold his gaze. Levi, the boy who I've spent the last six months avoiding because everyone wanted us to fall in love like some trope from a romance novel, wants in.

"You really don't need to be," I insist.

"Actually, Abbey, I kind of do. Kat warned me about your rather... err... impulsive tendencies. And to be honest.... you've always come across as a..." He pauses, opening one of the barren cupboards but doesn't finish.

"Come across as what?"

He hesitates and tries to hide his building smile."A control freak."

"Pfft, I am not. Let me guess, Kat also told you how I haven't had sex in over a year, and this is why you're helping me? To coax me into bed?"

He laughs. "You're beautiful, Abbey; I mean that sincerely, but I'm not interested in women."

"Wait...you're gay?" I stammer, nearly dropping the carton of milk in my hand.

"Since I was eleven years old."

Of course, he was. It all made perfect sense now. His soft-hearted nature, perfectly shaped brows, and love of book boyfriend-typed novels. All his kindness he'd shown me right down to the double-shot lattes he'd go out of his way to get me—it was never flirting. All this time, I'd pushed him away, afraid of giving him mixed messages when all he wanted to be was my friend.

CHAPTER NINE

PRESENT - JUNE

I'm awoken by the sound of a train rattling in the distance. It's four am, and to my right, I see Abbey curled up under one of my mother's infamous crocheted blankets, and next to her, with his head resting on her shoulder, is a younger gentleman who stirs, hearing me wake.

"Hey," he whispers, lifting his right arm to give me a wave.

"Should I know you?" I ask.

He gives me a sympathetic look. "No, this is the first time we've met."

"Well, that's good. You had me worried for a sec. What's your name?"

"Levi. I work with Abbey."

My eyes shift back to Abbey. Her hair is no longer tied back, lying in loose waves over her shoulders. In a way, it suits her, making her look more like the twenty-something-year-old she is instead of a woman approaching her forties. "She'll be cold under that old thing. Let me get her another blanket."

I stand and walk across to the linen cupboard, pulling down a feathered queen duvet and spreading it across them both.

"How are you feeling?" Levi asks. "Sounds like yesterday was an eventful day."

"I'll take it she told you."

He nods. "Not all of it. Just some."

"Tell me, does she have many friends? I can't work out why she is so..." I pause, trying to think of the right word. "Insistent?"

"Who, Abbey? Not really. Since her kid and partner died, she's been a bit of a loner. Everyone's tried to get her to go out on dates and live her life, but I can't decide if she's scared of moving on or feels guilty for even considering it."

"Maybe a bit of both," I say under my breath.

"Maybe. You know, I've never met someone like her. She's kind, almost to a fault. Before today, we'd barely spoken, but watching her, you get a sense she just wants to find a place in the world to call home."

"Don't we all?"

He laughs, the sound surprisingly animated and unselfconscious. "She means well."

"Yes, well, now, I'm not sure how to get rid of her." I sink into my chair and let out a long-winded sigh. For a while, we sit in silence. I expect him to say more, perhaps offer insight on how to detach myself from Abbey's well-intended grasp, but he doesn't. Instead, his eyes stay fixed on me for too long, and a sudden surge of nerves spreads through me. Silence has never made me uncomfortable, but with Levi obviously more at ease with the silence between us than I am, I realise for the first time I am.

"My grandfather had Alzheimer's," he finally says. "I wouldn't wish it on anybody."

"Neither would I. There's one thing to die as nature intended. Alzheimer's, it doesn't feel like nature or a rite of passage out of this world. I must've really pissed someone off because I can't think of any reason someone would do this to me."

"Are you scared?"

"I...I guess I am."

He looks down at his hands. "My grandfather, he never looked outwardly scared about the prognosis, but in secret, he tried to take his life a few times unsuccessfully."

"Maybe he wanted you to remember him for who he was, not what Alzheimer's made him become."

"Ironic because it's now all I remember." His gaze lifts, and he swipes his eyes. "Sorry. I don't know why I'm telling you all of this."

I do. There's a concept science can never explain. In moments of tragedy and times, we are drawn to others whose experience entwines with our own. Far beyond the endless pills and therapies designed to mask the darkness life creates, the best medicine of all is talking. It always has been.

So, I let Levi talk until the sun has risen and birds start to serenade the world with their song. He tells me how much his grandfather's death affected him and how his grandmother will never be the same. "In his final moments, he believed she was his first love," he admits. "My grandmother used to dismiss it as nothing more than gibberish but now has to live with all the unanswered questions. Whether, despite four decades together, he ever loved her as much as he'd loved her. She's a strong woman, one of the most formidable forces I know, but it's weakened her. No matter how much she tries to tell herself he didn't mean it, part of her knows he did."

"He would've loved her in his own way," I reassure. "Love is complex because no two are the same. I'm not sure if Abbey told you, but before all of this, I was a psychologist. If love was simple, I wouldn't have made a career out of helping people navigate its many layers. Sometimes, we lose someone before we're ready, and when that happens, it's so easy to hold on to a memory you've created. You wipe out the bad, smooth out the imperfections, and think it all would've been grand, because deep down, you wanted it to be perfect. You want to justify the hurt and the feelings of deep longing the separations created. It's more or less like a book. You've read half, maybe three-quarters of it and never get to read the ending. Without that finality, you always feel a sense of what could've been. Maybe had his first love not died, they would've gone on and lived a wonderful life. But at the same time, maybe they would've crashed and burned along the way. There's no knowing, and that, Levi, is what gets people the most—the what if."

• • • •

ABBEY WAKES SHORTLY before eight and is surprised to find Levi is up, cooking us breakfast, and I'm reading the latest Lee Child novel.

"What time is it?" she stammers, blinking herself awake.

"Nearly eight."

"Why didn't you wake me?"

"You were fast asleep."

She sits up and glances at the kitchen. "Sorry. Levi was at Tesco, too, and offered me a ride," she hisses under her breath. "I never expected him to stay."

"It's fine, no harm done. I must say, your shopping list was impressive, though I'm not sure why on earth you thought I needed these." I pick up the packet of bladder controls from the floor and fling them at her.

Her face reddens. "I don't even know how old you are—"

"Clearly my looks are doing me dirty then if you think I need those," I interrupt, laughing.

"You don't look old." She glances over at the kitchen before her eyes come back to mine. "I just...well...I've never done this before."

"Hungry?" Levi calls out, popping his head around the corner.

"Starving," Abbey admits.

"Same here," I add.

"Good because there's lots here."

We watch as he disappears again, and Abbey reaches for her phone. "Do you have a doctor?"

"I do. Several of them."

"What are their names?"

I can see her mind working double time, trying to come up with every possible question she should ask. "Not this again. I told you last night, I'm fine."

"You're not fine, and I can't leave here without knowing you'll be okay. If something happened to you, June, I'd never forgive myself."

People say that so often, and yet, I sense she's telling the truth. I can envision her, years from now, unable to let it go. She couldn't save me from myself. She'd replay every situation, each conversation and question she asked till she's built an impenetrable web of theories, each one further away from the truth.

"I'm really not your problem," I say. "Don't you have a million other things to do?"

"Lucky for you, I don't."

I keep my thoughts remaining on her. It would be easy to chalk her insistence to infatuation, maybe a desperation to do something notable in the world. Abbey, however, doesn't strike me as someone who was after glorification.

Levi admitted she'd lived a recluse lifestyle since the death of her family. She went to work and went home. There were no normal activities a woman in her twenties should be enjoying. No bar hopping, casual sex, or nights where her recollection is hazy. She'd never travelled or made plans other than to live the life she was merely existing in now. Maybe, like me, Abbey is lonely, and we are drawn to each other like magnets, speaking a language no other can see or hear.

"After breakfast, I'll let you speak to Michael. My neurologist."

She raises her brow. "Really?"

"Yes, really. He's been working with me for over a year. If it helps get you to leave me on my tod, I'll give you five minutes with him."

Her whole demeanour softens, and she smiles. For a second, I question if she is moments away from hugging me when Levi walks in carrying a plate of buttered toast.

"Right, ladies, at the table please," he says with a hint of authority woven into his voice.

CHAPTER TEN

ABBEY - PRESENT

After we've finished our breakfast, Levi leaves to get his grandmother off to a chiropractic appointment, and I am once again alone with June. She appears in good spirits and coherent, telling me how she thought she might go to her hometown for a few days. She'd been raised in a small fishing village in Ireland, and of all the places she'd visited in the world, no other place had made her feel at peace.

"I haven't been back there in years," she admits, rinsing her plate. "But I thought it would be good for me. You know, escape this rat race for a few days."

"Do you think you'll be okay to go alone?" I pause. "What if you get confused again?"

"When I'm on my tod, I have a system to bring me back to reality. It's worked for the most part."

I want to ask her what if it doesn't. You don't have to look very far to hear horror stories of Alzheimer's patients who have gotten themselves lost, fallen down cliffs, or died from hypothermia.

"You can go if Michael says it's a good idea," I say, turning so she can't read the uncertainty on my face.

She laughs. "When did you become my ma?"

"When you said I couldn't get anyone else involved."

"You've already broken that by involving Levi."

"Levi doesn't count," I say, folding my arms across my chest.

"Doesn't he? Well, neither does Michael."

"He's your doctor."

"Correction: he was my doctor."

"So, what is he now, then?"

"A friend," she says, opening the cupboard under the sink. She pulls out a tea towel and hands it to me. "Contrary to what you think, I do have them."

June speaks to Michael for a little over ten minutes after shutting herself in her bedroom. I walk up the stairs, hoping to get a hint of their discussion but fail miserably. The old cedar doors and heavy plaster walls soundproof everything into an indistinguishable murmur, and when she exits, she has an amused expression.

"Here," she says, handing me the phone. "You can use my bedroom."

I nod and take the phone. "Hi," I say, walking into the room. It's more abstract than I expected. The walls are coloured with a vivid Nordic blue, complimented by a distressed canary yellow dresser and side tables. There are dozens of photos and contemporary artwork from every corner, and it smells like vanilla incense and Chanel perfume.

"Hi," Michael replies as I shut the door. "Abbey, is it?"

"That's right."

"June has told me so much about you."

I bet she has.

"Good things, I hope."

He laughs without answering. "Did you have some things you wanted to talk about?"

I hesitate. Deep down, I want to tell him about the bridge and June's sudden lapse of memory at the restaurant, but there's a fear that if I do, he'll commit her when June doesn't want that, and neither do I.

"I'm worried about June," I admit before telling him about her plans to travel to Ireland. I ask him if he feels she is up for it and find myself surprised when he says he thinks she is.

"She has her days, no doubt, but I'm sure you've gathered her days are numbered. June's Alzheimer's is complex. I've seen patients be fully self-sufficient to need round-the-clock care within a month. But I trust her judgement. She's an incredibly smart woman, and I have no reason to believe she'd put herself in harm's way."

He clearly doesn't know about the bridge incident, then.

"So, you have no concerns at all?"

"No..." he replies, his voice tainted with uncertainty. "Unless, of course, I should have a reason to worry."

I shift the conversation. "Em, how long have you known June?"

"A little over two years. Why do you ask?"

"Has she...has she ever acted irrationally?"

"Not that I can think of. A little heated and spicy at times. Irrational? Not at all."

"I took her out for dinner last night, and she...lost her sense of where she was."

My confession doesn't seem to upset him, and he keeps his speech well-constructed. "Interesting. She never told me that."

"She wouldn't. You know her," I say, making it sound like I've known her longer than he has. "Her pride is her biggest downfall."

"I guess that's normal. She was in here a while ago after losing her bearings during a run. I didn't know there had been other episodes."

"There haven't." Trying to recover control of the situation, I lie, uncertain whether it comes across as believable or as transparent as it feels.

"That's good. She tells me your mother was an old friend."

All the moisture in my mouth evaporates in seconds, and I feel there's cotton wool stuffed inside. "Uh...yes, that's right."

"It's nice for me to hear that. She gave me the impression she didn't have anyone."

"She does," I lie again. "More than she realises."

"That's great."

The line goes silent, with neither of us knowing whether to further or end the conversation. Inside, I have so many questions. From when he thought she'd need assisted living to whether there were any carer facilities available to her. In the end, I don't ask them, and Michael cuts the conversation by stating he has an appointment to get to. June is sitting at the dining table, reading the newspaper, when I head back down the stairs.

"You lied to him," I say, handing the phone to her. "A family friend?"

"It sounds less concerning than the truth, doesn't it?"

"I guess. A little pre-warning would have been nice, though."

"I'm sure you handled it just fine," she says, unfazed.

She turns the page and looks up at me. "What did he say about my trip?"

"That he thought you'd be fine. The thing is, you didn't tell him about the restaurant or the bridge."

"Why would I? They were minor lapses in judgement. It happens and will continue to happen."

I shake my head. "You're not going."

She folds the paper closed, keeping her eyes fixed in my direction. "Excuse me?"

"What if you fall off a cliff or worse, take a plane to a foreign country."

"Right now, that sounds delightful."

"Not funny," I say, pulling a face. "I'm coming with you."

"Why would you do that? And better yet, why do you think I'd even allow it?"

I shrug. "You said I might find someone travelling. Why not kill two birds with one stone? You get your trip, and I get a chance to find a dapper, handsome Irishman."

She laughs. "Trust me, you won't be finding anything dapper in my neck of the woods."

"You said you haven't been in over a decade. Things might've changed."

"Some places, just like people, never change."

I shrug again. "Well, I've never left England, so I have nothing to judge it from."

"You've *never* left England."

"Nope."

"Okay, fine. We'll leave this weekend."

"Are you serious?"

"Of course, I'm serious, Abbey. Don't ask too many questions, and dress appropriately, and we'll be fine."

"Dress appropriately? What's wrong with my clothes?"

She doesn't answer me and points to her phone. "Put your number in there, and we'll go shopping tomorrow. Life is for living, Abbey; you ought to start dressing like it."

• • • •

THE NEXT DAY, IT'S finally stopped snowing, and I'm enjoying my morning coffee in the sun when Levi stops in the doorway to my office. "You got a sec?"

"Sure." I look past his shoulder and see Kat watching us. "Come in and close the door behind you."

"How's June?"

"Good," I say, standing to close the door.

"I've been thinking, and I can't work it out. Have you always been so introverted?"

His question catches me off-guard. How can you explain to a normal person that two versions of you exist in the world? One who hadn't been touched by tragedy and the other who is now a walking version of it. "Eh. Honestly, no. I actually used to like people."

"June must be different then, right? She's a stranger, and you treat her like she's a friend."

I walk over to my desk without looking at him. "I worry about her."

"Or maybe you aren't as introverted as you thought."

"You can not like people and still care about people. They aren't the same things."

He takes a seat. "No, see, here's what I think. You're scared to be close to people. It's not that you don't want to; it's that you feel like you can't."

Where's this coming from?

"You spent a few hours with me, and that's what you gathered?"

"Let's just say you aren't as reserved as you think you are. I see you, Abbey. For what it's worth, I see you. Maybe from a distance, I always have."

I roll my eyes. "You're quoting one of your books now."

"If I was quoting my books, it'd be far more poetic."

"You haven't told anyone, have you?"

"Of course, I haven't."

"Good," I say, sinking into my chair.

"What happens now?"

"Honestly, I don't know. I spoke to her doctor this morning, and he seems to think she's fine."

"A woman who nearly jumped off a bridge is fine?"

"Well, she hasn't told him that, obviously."

"I hope you told him?"

He phrases it like a question and statement all in one, and I hesitate, unsure whether now would be a time to lie.

"Abbey, really?"

"It isn't my place to say anything," I stammer.

"I'd argue it also isn't your place to become this woman's caregiver. Forty-eight hours ago, you two were nothing more than strangers."

"You're starting to sound like her."

"Do you not reckon it's because we are right?"

"I'm taking her to Ireland at the weekend, and then I'll sort out some care for her."

"You're *what*? You don't know this woman."

"And what better way to get to know her? Look, I don't expect you to get it, but at least respect my decisions."

"Are you listening to yourself?" He shakes his head, and for the life of me, I can't understand why he seems riled by my admission. "You're taking her to another country and saying you'll sort care. She isn't your mother, Abbey. There are people, trained professionals that are equipped to deal with these exact situations."

"I promised her I wouldn't interfere without her consent."

"Fuck the promise. This isn't some fairytale. You could both get hurt." He pauses. "If this is about Scott and some self-righteous vendetta to help her because you feel guilty, you have nothing to prove, Abbey. You hear me? Nothing. None of it was your fault."

"Please, leave," I whisper. Part of me wants to yell at him and scream how he has no idea what he's talking about, but there's a part of me that's conflicted, questioning if what he said is true.

I couldn't explain the forces at work pulling me towards June, wanting to protect her from the pain and inevitable confusion awaiting her. There were no words to describe how, in her presence, I feel a sense of belonging. Then there are the questions of why, which visit me by the hour, ones I have no answer to.

I thought I'd gained closure for all I couldn't do when it came to Scott. All the hurt, betrayal, and self-inflicted punishment for my momentary lapse of judgement, which derailed our lives, have long ceased and dried. But what if I hadn't? What if, like June, I'd lied to the outside world till it became my truth? What if my soul longs to help her because, in a selfish way, it needs to?

As I watch Levi leave, hooking a left and then disappearing from sight, the question of why revisits me once more, only this time, I can feel the truth peeling from beneath, almost close enough to view.

CHAPTER ELEVEN

JUNE - PRESENT

I spend the day at home, packing when I suddenly become exhausted. I must've fallen asleep as I wake up with a dry throat and a head that feels like it's been hit by a double-decker bus. But suddenly, it dawns on me that I don't know how I got here. I know I'm at home, which does little to soothe my growing panic.

What was I doing? What day of the week is it?

I stand, panning my surroundings. There's a suitcase half-closed next to me and a clip-lock bag with a passport and a pair of sunglasses.

Am I going somewhere?

From beneath me, I hear a radio playing Bob Dylan, and then my ears tune into a different sound—a phone ringing.

Shit. Abbey!

I scramble and make my way for the door, only it isn't the door; it's my wardrobe. I make the same mistake not once but twice, and on the third attempt, I open my ensuite door. It's happened before more than once; each time, however, I was back within minutes. This time feels different, like I've reached another checkpoint in the twisted game alzheimer's has made of my life.

There's nothing but tears and audible panic escaping me in a series of primitive sounds. Desperate and helpless, a sound rattles through my bones, squeezing every pint of blood from my veins. "Wake up," I scream, rocking back and forth once my body hits the floor. "Please, let me wake up."

By the time I've come to my senses, I'm over thirty minutes late to meet Abbey. She's sitting at the café, checking her phone anxiously and looks like someone seconds away from leaving.

"Hey," I mumble, pulling out the chair next to her.

"I was worried."

"Worried I'd forgotten?"

She studies me for a moment. "No. Just worried."

"Sorry, I missed the bus here and had to wait for the next one."

"It's fine." She finishes her coffee, and I can tell from her averted gaze and tight-lipped expression that something is bothering her.

"Bad day?"

"You could say that."

"Do you want to talk about it?"

"If by talking you mean telling me how crazy I am for sitting here with you right now, I think I'll pass."

"Well, you aren't crazy, for starters. Eccentric, yes. A little impulsive, but I'd be more inclined to say well-intentioned."

"I'm glad you think so."

"I take it Levi does?"

"He thinks this is some selfish and poorly thought-out attempt at forgiving myself."

"And it's not?'

She pulls a face as if I've offended her. "Of course, it isn't."

"I wouldn't judge you if it was."

"Good to know," she says, staring at her empty mug. "Do you want a coffee, or should we get going?"

"We can go."

We take the bus to the West End and make our way to Oxford Street. The streets are slowly winding down from the day, and the buskers are packing up their guitars, counting each penny they've made. Abbey isn't in the mood to talk. She keeps her head low and appears lost in a space neither here nor there. I want to press it but opt not to and take to smoking my cigarette, savouring each nicotine-infused drag.

"You shouldn't smoke those things," she says without looking at me.

"I'm dying, anyway."

"I take it you aren't an organ donor, then."

I laugh, and a steady stream of smoke escapes my lips. "Nobody would want my organs."

She slows her step as we approach an intersection. "For everyone willing to donate an organ, there are four people who desperately need one."

"Well, that's one wretched way to look at it."

We head into a lingerie shop first, which I can tell makes Abbey uncomfortable. She doesn't know where to look, and her cheeks have flushed pink.

"I'm going to take a wild guess you wear beige padded bras from Primark," I say, pulling out a sheer camisole.

"Close. But not beige; they're white."

"Well, I'm buying you a set or two, three if you feel so inclined."

"You aren't buying me anything."

"I can't take money to the grave with me. Today is on me—all of it."

She pulls out a maroon-red underwire and brief set, and her eyes scan the price tag. "Absolutely not."

"Come on," I say, focusing on her bust. She looked about a C-cup, give or take, and a rough thirty in the band. "Otherwise, I'll just pick for you."

"Why are you so focused on my underwear?"

"You said so yourself; you want to woo an Irishman. What happens if you find one, and he takes you home only to find you've raided his mam's knicker drawer?"

Her cheeks redden further, and she glances down the aisles to see if anyone heard me. "Could you speak any louder?"

"Could you be any more of a pain in the arse?"

She shakes her head and pulls out another set. It's black and embroidered with a light pink lace trim.

"I like that one," I say, watching as she awkwardly holds it to her chest. "Pair it with some suspenders, a tight black dress, and heels. You'd be good to go."

"I'd look like a lady of the night."

"Maybe, but if you've got it, flaunt it."

For a second, she looks as if she is about to put it back, and then, to my surprise, she hands it to me. "Okay. Just this one."

Her face gives it away. The small vote of confidence is all she needed, and half an hour later, we walk out of the store with a half-dozen sets each and head on to the next store.

It's nearing six when we head to a local small boutique eatery with our arms full of bags and me one transaction away from the bank's fraud department calling. I'm surprised that after this morning's incident, I've managed to stay relatively coherent other than a minor slip up, forgetting the pin number to my Visa, which, luckily, I had written in my book. And after Abbey's disgruntled attitude at the start, she's also smiling.

Some people lack the ability to smile without looking oddly maniacal and deranged. Abbey, however, her smile is one of her most attractive features. It spreads from each corner, scrunching her eyes and imprinting fine wrinkles across her nose. But most of all, it's infectious to anyone lucky enough to lay their eyes upon it.

We slide into our seats, and Abbey reaches across for a menu. "I have to admit, that was fun."

"We'll have to do it again when we get back from Ireland," I say.

"I'd like that."

A waitress comes and takes our drinks order, and this time, I opt for juice.

Abbey looks across at me, amused. "No tequila, then?"

"I'll save it for this weekend." I wink. In truth, I'm concerned drinking brings on the memory lapses more frequently and hoped Abbey wouldn't see through my less-than-desirable dishonesty skills. It works because she doesn't bat an eye and shifts the conversation back to Craig and me.

"Have you ever thought about finding him?"

"Where is this coming from?"

She shrugs. "I dunno. I guess with your diagnosis and all."

"I doubt he would want to know."

"And you never moved on?"

"I tried to. Had sex with a lot of strangers and put myself into situations I now regret. All it did was make me miserable when I realised the void of not having him in my life was one I'd never be able to fill."

"At least you've done better than me," she says, trailing the lip of her glass. "I've only slept with Scott. I wouldn't know what to do with anyone else."

"You will with the right person."

"How do you even know?"

"Because," I say. "I came close to it."

Five years after Craig and I divorced, my path crossed with Harrison, a recently widowed detective with the local police. Ethically, dating patients is wrong, so despite our evident connection and shared a mutual love of classical literature, I shelved it, and he eventually relocated to Wales to be closer to his adult son and grandchildren.

Our paths wouldn't cross for another year when we attended the wedding of a mutual friend. I knew from the moment I saw him, dressed in his dark navy suit and yellow tie, he was the closest thing to Craig I'd ever felt. His presence calmed me, and each move his body made when it became at one with mine set me on fire. I could've loved him; if I had allowed myself to.

Even after all these years, I reflect on why it scared me so much. Was it because I feared moving on from Craig tarnished all we had and all I'd given away? Or was it simpler than that? In a way, I felt I deserved to be punished. And it hits me, staring at Abbey, it's like looking in the mirror at my own reflection, not because of our looks or how our eyes speak of the same sadness woven in a different way, but because we both are yearning to forgive ourselves without a clue as to how.

CHAPTER TWELVE

ABBEY - PRESENT

It's Friday. I've taken the day off since June wants to leave the city by mid-afternoon, and I'm still nursing a mild hangover from days prior when I receive a phone call from Scott's mother.

When he died, she sold everything and decided to backpack around the world. As he was an only child and she'd raised him single-handedly, without him, all purpose in her life disintegrated. She was labelled mad and lost many of her closest friends, but in the end, she flourished. For those around her that were divorced, relationships with their children became forced, but by finding a deep-rooted love for the world around her, Scott's mother achieved a feat few do. She became unapologetically in love with life.

"Abbey," she says the moment I answer. She must be at a beach; I can hear gulls in the background and the murmur of voices.

"Helen. How are you?"

"I am doing fantastic. You must come visit. Croatia in the summer, there's nothing like it."

"One day, I just might."

"Please do." She pauses, and her voice turns more serious, "I don't want to bring this up, Abbey, but we really need to think about giving Scott an unveiling. It's been over a year. I know it isn't something either of us think about, but the last week, all I've been thinking is how he's just sitting there. I can fly back, and we can have a small ceremony. Maybe invite some of the family, some friends of you both."

My stomach twists. I hadn't spoken to any of our so-called friends in months.

"Helen," I begin, without knowing what to say next. "I...now isn't a good time. I...I just..." I cut myself short. The last thing I needed was her knowing about June or how I don't feel ready when the world is trying to convince me I should be.

"If it's too hard for you, I can organise it. You don't even have to come."

"No!" I stammer. "Look, can you just give me another month or two? I promise before his birthday, we'll have it done."

"His birthday is six weeks away." She says it so matter of fact that I can almost taste the scepticism in her words. I can't blame her. It's the fifth time we've had this conversation, and not once have we come closer to getting it resolved. In all fairness, it wasn't that I hadn't tried—quite the opposite. Four times I've tried to plan his headstone, and twice, I'd reached the point of calling about them. But the one time I made an appointment to go, I got to the car park of the home and couldn't go inside as the radio started playing our wedding song that I contrived as a sign I wasn't ready yet.

Madness, I know, but his absence has created its own language in me; one few understand, and only I have the ability to speak.

"I promise you, I'm ready this time."

Helen goes quiet, and through the receiver, I can't tell whether she likes my answer or if she even believes it. "Please come visit me. A holiday could be good for you," she finally says before we say our goodbyes, and she hangs up.

By midmorning, I'm packed, and whether spurred by my conversation with Helen or a subconscious fear of flying has spurred it, I decide to go to the cemetery. With Aila's urn in my bag, I make the twenty-minute walk in silence, picking up a single customary can of Foster's that Scott once loved. It has been months since I visited. Partly because it was easier to live in a world where the reminder of Scott was a story I could manipulate for my own comfort, and the other part is because revisiting his grave drives the realisation he's never coming back. It's unexplainable to me how, when it comes to Aila, my experience couldn't be more different. Science talks about the bond mothers have with their offspring, formed when mother and child are two parts of the same being. But it's deeper than many of us realise. I knew the minute she left me because the coil that once linked us seized, and with it, the energy supply connecting us switched off. Where I once felt her, there was nothing but an infinite void, as if the minute she left this world, I broke in two, and she took half of me with her. It made it easier to grieve for her, but at the same time, stirred so many questions of guilt as to why I could let her go but not him.

It's empty when I exit the car, with only the autumn leaves falling like rain around me for company. I hook a left and follow the long line of graves before taking a right down his row. He's the only one without a stone. Surrounded by granite and marble, the smoothed mound of dirt is all that makes known of his existence.

"Hey," I whisper, sitting cross-legged on the ground. I place Aila down next to me and take a deep breath before closing my eyes.

It's been a religious practice of mine that when I talk to him, I can't look. As crazy as it may seem, behind the safety of darkness, I can almost bring him back to life. Sometimes, it's as simple as a faint outline in an illusionary sunset. Other times, I can breathe life into the warmth of his embrace. I know none of it is real, but with the outside world shut away, I give myself the grace to believe it is.

I wait in silence, my ears tuned into the soft rustle of leaves from behind me, but he doesn't visit me today—Aila does. She's no longer a baby as she sits opposite me with her hair parted in plaits. Her eyes are still a carbon copy of her father's, but the rest of her looks like me. From her delicate cheekbones to her expressive brows, staring at her is like I've painted a toddler portrait of myself. I can feel the tears falling, but I don't wipe them. Too scared that if I move her, I'll lose my vision of her, I sit still, hoping she'll come closer. But she doesn't. Instead, she stands and smiles at me.

"Please," I whisper, my tears turning into a deluge. "Just a little longer."

She shakes her head, playfully giggling.

"Aila, please. Please, don't go."

I'm acutely aware of the words coming out of my mouth, but the urge to keep her is stronger.

"Please," I say again. But it's too late. She dissolves right before my eyes, and nothing within my power can hold back the scream.

For a while, I rock back and forth, sobbing with my knees tucked in tight. I used to fear being forgotten, but now, all I fear is being remembered. Remembering is what hurts. It's the remembering that shackles me inside until I'm screaming to be let free. I don't regret our life, not even for a second, but I'd be lying if I said there wasn't a large piece of me wishing I could forget.

"Hey, stranger."

Suddenly, I feel a hand on my back, and my eyes fly open, seeing Levi crouched down next to me.

I wipe my face, not daring to look at him. "What are you doing here?"

"I could ask you the same thing."

I nod with my eyes closed, desperate to stop the tears from resurfacing but it's impossible.

"Hey...Abbey, don't...don't cry," he says, pulling me into his chest. "If you must know, I was visiting my father. Today would've been his birthday."

The way he holds me isn't like a stranger or a colleague I've shared limited conversation with. He pulls me in like he's shielding me from raining gunfire, and it's enough for me to unravel completely. By the time I look up again, I don't know how much time has passed, but my hair has glued itself to Levi's cheek, and his eyes look redder than mine.

"Come on, you," he finally says. "Let's take a walk."

CHAPTER THIRTEEN

ABBEY - PRESENT

After placing the urn in his car, Levi and I take the loop down to the Thames. It's deserted, minus a couple walking their pint-sized dog and two women clad in activewear running like a pair of galloping horses down the bridle path. We take a seat on a bench overlooking the break wall, and Levi offers me a cigarette.

"Not you, too," I say. "You and June really shouldn't smoke those things."

He pulls out one, placing it between his lips and laughs. "I don't smoke often. Just on days like today."

"You said you were visiting your father, right?"

He nods, lighting the end. "Well, he was really my grandfather. But I was raised by him and my nan. My parents aren't in the picture and never have been."

"I'm sorry."

"Don't be. They made the right choice." He pauses and leans back, letting out a deep exhalation of smoke that twists and turns through the air. "You want to talk about why you are in such a state?"

I force a smile. "I'm not now."

He studies me, drawing in another deep inhale before releasing it. "You're a terrible liar...or should I say, actress?"

"Maybe I'm both."

"Maybe you are. Still, I'm here as a friend—no judgement."

I let out a sigh, eyeing him for a moment. "Do you believe in the afterlife?"

"If I say no, would you hold it against me?"

"Not in the slightest."

"Then no," he says, "I don't."

"I wanted to believe it so bad. For months after she died, I'd sit in her room all hours of the night, drifting in and out of sleep, hoping that one day, when I woke up, it'd all be a dream. Sounds crazy when I say it now, but there were nights I was so sleep-deprived I'd hear her crying. It seemed...so real...and then, I'd open the door, only to find the room empty.

"I thought, if it existed, heaven that is, why would nobody let me know she was safe? Why would they let me drive myself to the point of mania when all I needed to do was see her? You know, you hear all these stories about people feeling things or seeing their loved ones who have crossed over and I never saw her, not once. And then what's even crazier, I told myself maybe whoever controls such things was protecting me. But if that's the case, why do I see Scott? Why do I see him everywhere and not her? How is that fair?"

Levi moves closer and places a gentle arm around me.

"I hate him. I hate him, Levi but I still....I still love him. He was horrible to me towards the end and here I am, still in love with someone and he's not even here to know it."

Do you ever get over losing someone without a reason why? Or do you just find a way to bury it deep within yourself, deep enough so it'd take an internal landslide of catastrophic proportions to resurface it? I thought that maybe if I dug down to the pain inside and shovelled enough self-loathing and unanswered questions on top, it would surrender on its own. As foolish as it sounds, I thought maybe, just maybe, I'd one day visit the burial spot and unearth it all, to find everything I'd been carrying with me was gone. Now, I know nothing could be further from the truth.

"You always will, Abbey. There's no shame in that."

I shake my head. "But there is. How can I have a life with someone else if all I want is my life back with him?"

"Do you want that? A life with someone else?"

"Some days, yes," I pause and stare down at my hands, lacing them together. "I mean...I don't want to be alone for the rest of my life."

I wish it didn't hurt me to say it. I wish that my love for Scott wasn't so controlling and ubiquitous. But that's not very realistic, is it? When you love someone the way I loved him, it forms an identity in you. Then the day comes for it to end, and you find yourself not just grieving for the life you had but mourning for the person you once were who died in the aftermath.

In the year that has passed, I've found myself caught in a riptide of wanting to let her go—the ghost of me who lingers from our life together. When each time I get close, another wave comes, and I get dragged under again, believing a part of me will always remain hollow if I do.

"Do me a favour, close your eyes and tell me how your life looks ten years from now."

"Right here?"

"Yes, right here."

"I—"

"Just do it. Don't think about it."

"Okay," I say, closing my eyes.

Levi grabs my hand, and behind the shield of darkness, I listen to the river and the sounds of starlings in the distance.

It takes a while for the picture to come together, fuzzy at first; I see myself through a half-opened window staring at a barren Xmas tree. I never see my face or the way my skin looks after a life lived alone, but as I watch my silhouette take a seat with a photograph in hand, I realise it feels like I'm watching myself in June's shoes, alone and afraid, searching for the last remaining place that feels like home.

I open my eyes again and wipe my face when I realise I've been crying again.

"So, how did it look?"

"Not great," I whisper.

"Can we change it?"

I stare at him, unsure if I heard him correctly. "We?"

"I told you, I'm here as a friend."

"Can't say I've had many experiences with those," I say under my breath.

"Maybe if you didn't push people away, you'd see so many of us have wanted to get to know you, Abbey. Everyone needs a friend, even people like you who think they hate people."

"I never said I hate people."

"You didn't have to. Your face says it for you."

I pull a face. "Well, thanks?"

He smiles and releases my hand. "So, you're really doing this trip with June?"

"She needs me."

"You know, my grandfather had dementia. The difference was, his body was already in the process of giving up before it began. June, she's so young in comparison." He reaches for another cigarette. "I worry you'll find yourself in a situation with a woman who is physically able but mentally isn't. You've never been around someone with the condition. It can change quicker than the weather here in a day."

"It's just a weekend."

"Is it?" He lifts his left hand, cupping his cigarette so he can light it. "I think both you and I know that is a lie—which you and I know you're shockingly bad at."

I stare at the end of his cigarette, focusing on how the embers all have different shades of red when he inhales.

"Have you ever asked yourself how this ends?"

"She'll go to a supported living facility, of course."

"But that, from what I remember, isn't what she wants?"

"So, what you're saying is I should've let her jump?" I fire back, folding my arms.

"That isn't what I'm saying at all. Look, all I'm saying is, maybe you and June, if you're going to continue this...thing...whatever it is, maybe you two need to discuss what happens now. There will come a time when she wants to end it again, and I don't want to see you hurt when that day comes."

I know his concern is genuine, and perhaps, in a way, I worry, too, about how I will cope when it does eventually end. I saved June's life once, but I'd be lying if I said there were parts of me convinced that if it came to round two, the outcome might not be the same.

CHAPTER FOURTEEN

JUNE - PRESENT

In my mother's final month of life, she brought to life the concept that when you lose one sense, the others become superhuman. She could smell a bakery three blocks away in a single gust of wind and hear the sound of a tap dripping halfway down the corridor after wearing hearing aids for years. I'm old enough to know life and death are two things which are inevitable in life, and seeing it first hand, in all of its enigmatic states, I realised how remarkable and scientifically unexplainable the last days we write in the world are.

Two days before she passed away, I came to visit her to find her deep in discussion with her brother, who'd died in a tragic accident walking home from a pub one evening on the eve of his twenty-second birthday. For a while, I watched her. She was laughing and sharing tales of things she'd never told me, like how she and George brewed their own whisky in one of the farm sheds and his failed attempt to find her a good husband. But to the naked eye, there was nobody there.

It was easy to believe it was her mind short-circuiting and breathing to life conversations deep within her subconscious layers she longed to have. Then, I smelt him. After moving from my doorway post, I walked around the right side of her bed, and suddenly, my nostrils filled with the distinct sweet smell of rum-cured tobacco. My mother never smoked, and I knew from our limited conversations, George was never seen without a staple hand-rolled cigarette hanging out of his mouth. Maybe it was both of our minds playing tricks, but as a warm hand placed itself on my back, igniting a wildfire of goosebumps across my skin, there wasn't a doubt there weren't just two of us in the room that day; there were three.

Lately, I've started to feel it, too: someone watching me, waiting for the right time. It frightened me at first, and I found myself in a free-for-all panic that I wouldn't live to see the next morning, and now, it offers me comfort. It may be an illusion, another twisted game played by Alzheimer's hands, and without a pious bone in my body, I doubted the afterlife existed, but I'm starting to believe life doesn't end—at least, not the way we think it does.

After packing my bags for the trip, I'm disrupted by the sound of music echoing from downstairs, and I freeze. With the increasing unpredictability of my memory lapses, I'd been check-listing myself to switch everything off at the wall after one too many occasions of waking up in the middle of the night with my radio on full blast.

Had I forgotten?

Walking down the stairs, I feel a sense of dread, as if my mind is two steps ahead of me. I pause, listening to the sound. It's clear. There's no distortion, and I tell myself I must've just forgotten. It's okay; it happens. Then as I round the corner, I see my mother. She's sitting in the chair, which looks right into the doorway, staring at me with all the softness drained from her once-loving eyes.

"Ma?" I whisper.

"How could you, June?"

"I...I have no idea what you're talking about?"

"It's okay for you to do it, but not me? You let me suffer. Why?"

I know it's nothing more than an illusion, constructed by my own innermost thoughts, but I can't help the suffocation. It starts at the neck, wrapping itself around me till my breaths become a chain of ineffectual air, deflating my lungs like a pair of punctured tyres. Then it moves into my chest. The pain is searing, and then I taste it. It isn't the familiar metallic taste of blood or leftover morning espresso. As I fall to the floor, heaving for breath and gripping my chest, I know without a doubt what it is. It's death. The unmistakable and unsettling entree of approaching death.

"June?" I hear a woman's voice and blink myself awake. It takes me a moment once my eyes adjust to the light and my surroundings to realise it's Abbey. I must've fallen asleep as I'm lying on the bed with a scrunched-up shirt in my right hand and a half-packed suitcase to the left of me.

"Sorry," Abbey continues, walking into the room. "I tried calling."

"Don't you apologise," I say. "I must've been tired."

She nods and takes a seat next to me. "You know we can always go another time. It has been a full-on week for you."

"I'd rather go now."

"Okay," she says slowly. "I'm all ready to go when you are."

"I just need to make a quick phone call." I look at my half-filled suitcase and then back to Abbey. "Can you do me a favour and check what I've packed? I...I don't remember what I put in there."

"Of course." She smiles, and I excuse myself downstairs.

I'm careful what I say to Michael when I tell him about the nightmares. In truth, I can no longer distinguish between the two. If the dreams indeed are dreams, why are they so real?

"How frequent are they?"

"I don't exactly keep a tally of these things," I say, massaging the side of my neck. "Maybe every few days."

"Are you sleeping well?"

"Yes and no."

"What would you rate your sleep routine at the moment out of ten?"

"A four...maybe a five."

"And do you know when you are dreaming versus when you are awake?"

I swallow. "Uh...yeah...yeah, I do."

"I know you are very anti-medication, June, but there are things that could help. It isn't uncommon to experience nightmares, especially as Alzheimer's progresses." He pauses, clearing his throat. "We don't yet fully understand why they occur, but many patients I've seen over the last five years eventually have trouble separating the two."

"So, this is all...just normal behaviour."

"I'm afraid so."

I know the drug he wants to suggest; I've seen it used with a number of clients over the years to treat PTSD. It has its benefits, but like anything in life, there is always a balance which needs to be outweighed. Right now, that balance is still tipped in the negative.

"So, you're away this weekend, eh?" Michael continues on.

"Sure am."

"Do you have much planned?"

"Other than pretending I'm not losing it for a few days? No."

He laughs. “Okay. Well, I hope you two have fun. Call if you need me.”

“Do I need to remind you that you’re not my doctor anymore?”

“And yet, here you are.”

“What can I say, nobody gets me like you do.”

“And what can I say, I’m breaking every ethical rule imaginable, June, because it’s you. Take care and be safe.”

“Nowhere is safe,” I say, laughing. “Bye for now.”

I head back upstairs, and Abbey helps me pack the last of my things. Turns out, I’d packed for a visit to Hawaii, not the middle of winter. We laugh about it at first, but deep down, it unsettles me. Day-to-day things are becoming a challenge, and one day soon, I fear one of the last remaining things which makes me feel human will be too—my decisions. After we are all sorted and I have thrown on something a bit more climatised, we make our way downstairs and out to the car.

“Will you be okay to drive?” Abbey asks, placing our suitcases into the boot.

“I’m not that invalid yet,” I tease. “If somewhere along the way, I feel my mind playing tricks on me, you can just take over.”

She closes the boot, and her demeanour changes. Suddenly, it hits me.

“You haven’t driven since the accident, have you?”

“I mean...I’ve wanted to. I just...”

“It’s okay,” I reassure. “Worst case scenario, we’ll hitchhike.”

“Pfft, we are not hitchhiking anywhere.” She shakes her head, laughing. “I’ll be okay...if it comes to it, that is.”

I walk around to the driver's side and pause before I open the door. "Abbey," I say, glancing across at her.

She shoots me a look. "Yes?"

"I have two rules. First, don't touch the radio. Second, since you don't smoke and your window doesn't wind down, use the sunroof."

CHAPTER FIFTEEN

ABBEY - PRESENT

By the time we reach the outskirts of Birmingham, June's on her sixth cigarette, and I can almost feel the nicotine seeping into my bloodstream.

"How can you like those poisonous things?" I say, watching as she lights the end of number seven.

"We all need a self-inflicted poison in life. It's what makes life worth living."

"Making yourself die faster is what makes life worth living?"

She laughs, and a steady chain of smoke escapes her lips. "No. Being in control of your own mortality does. It's why some people do that," she says, gesturing to a woman power-walking up the footpath with a scruffy terrier jogging next to her. "I used to think it was the endorphins. That's what science tells us, right? But no. Dig a little deeper, Abbey, and you'll find it's the power it brings. Mortality is power, and between you and me, it's the one thing we have the slightest control over."

"I'm not sure I understand your logic."

"One day, you will."

I rest my head on the passenger window, watching as the droplets race against one another. "Why didn't we fly? You realise this is like a nine-hour trip?"

"Flying scares me."

"It's one of the safest modes of transport around."

"Clearly, you haven't been in a plane in the Atlantic and hit by turbulence that knocked out two flight attendants and injured a dozen passengers."

"No, you're right. Actually, don't laugh. I've never been on a plane."

She glances at me. "Never?"

"We planned it, but I guess...we never got to do it."

"Shame that. Funny how life works. Each choice we make is part of a much larger plan."

It would be easy to lay into her how insensitive her remark is when in a way, she's right. I consider for a moment what would have happened if I'd been standing just a little bit farther on the road that day. What if she'd jumped a few seconds earlier? Today might never have existed—at least, not how it is right now. How weird is that? The difference between life and death can be altered in seconds, and all the moments in between, changed by a single choice.

"Do you think about what would have happened? If...if I hadn't stopped you?"

"Not in the slightest." She leans forward, stubbing out her cigarette. "There lies your problem. Abbey, you're in your head too much."

"How can you not think about that? You—"

"I wouldn't be sitting here right now. Do us both a favour and try not to think about it. Think about us going to Egypt or something great."

"What are you talking about?"

"After this, we should go somewhere. One last hooray for me, and for you, a breaking of the seal."

I fall silent, and my thoughts drift to Scott. We'd never had the chance to travel even though it was something we always wanted to do. When I was seven months pregnant with Aila, Scott had just returned from a week-long stint in Dubai and suggested we go abroad.

"We need to go for a trip," he says, kneeling to kiss my ever-expanding stomach.

I burst into laughter. "A trip? We are just about to have a baby."

"I know. I mean, when she's old enough."

"You'll be waiting a long time."

"I'll wait as long as I need to." He grins.

I smile, running my hands through his hair. "Where were you thinking?"

He gives my stomach another kiss before standing. "Egypt first, of course. I mean, Abbey, I have to see it all up close." His eyes light up, and he walks into the kitchen. "There are so many places we have to go. Greece would be second on the list. Then, Italy."

"And where is this money coming from?"

"I can work remotely. Greg and I have already talked about it."

"Okay," I say, laughing. "Where would we live?"

"That's another thing Greg and I have talked about. See, our company has several employee vacation homes throughout. We would be able to stay in them for up to four weeks at a time." He shoots me a smile, opening the refrigerator door. "I have it planned. You just need to say yes."

I realise I've been sitting silent for too long when June presses a finger into my shoulder. "What is it, kiddo? You look like you've seen a ghost."

"It's nothing."

"Come on now. It's me you're talking to."

I swallow hard. "How do you do it? Move on, I mean. Everywhere I look, he's there."

"He always will be. I think most people get it wrong when it comes to grief. We try to bury the pain because it's what our natural instinct wants us to do. Thing is, pain is a symptom of being human, and acceptance only comes when we make peace with its existence." She reaches across for my hand. "And you know what the most messed up part about grieving is? There comes a time when we start to mourn for a life and a person that never existed. But it passes, Abbey. Like anything in life, it passes, and when it does, you'll see the world through lenses you never have before."

"I'm not convinced of that."

"Right now, you don't need to be."

"You're a terrible therapist, you know."

She laughs and nudges me on the shoulder. "Enlighten me. What did your 'good' therapist tell you?"

"I need to stop focusing on the past as my present doesn't live there."

"See that...that is rubbish advice. Sure, living in the past can be negative. On the contrary, nobody is ever able to fully give themselves to the present if the past is still in pieces. I best liken it to a jigsaw puzzle. We need to know what the picture looks like in order to grow and learn from our shortcomings. Otherwise, how else can we make sense of something and move forward?"

"I like your advice better."

"Well, good because you should."

• • • •

BY THE TIME WE REACH the ferry dock with our takeaway bags of McDonald's, the sun has set in the sky, and there are only long-haul truck drivers and two campers waiting to board. June has gone very quiet, staring out the window as if she's revisiting a painful memory.

"You okay?" I ask, taking a slow slurp of chocolate milkshake.

"I think so. You know, it's funny driving here. I remember things I never have before."

"In all fairness, you said it has been nearly a decade since you've made the journey. Sometimes, we forget things because, at the time, it doesn't seem important until one day, they are."

She playfully scowls. "Did you...did you just give me advice, Abbey?"

"Not at all. I don't give advice."

"Is that so..." She reaches into her bag and pulls out her pottle of chips. "Sounded an awful lot like advice to me."

I shrug. "If the shoe fits..."

"The last time I came here, it was to say goodbye to Craig. I'd loaded up the car to the brim, and I thought he wouldn't follow me, but—" She sighs and wipes her eyes. "In all the times I've been back, I always took the ferry from Wales. Could never bring myself to come here. The memory hurt too much. For some reason, I thought today would be different. This disease, Abbey, is making me relive so much. I...I don't even know why I'm telling you this."

"Because I'm your friend."

She looks across at me. "I don't do friends."

"Me neither. So, let's not be friends, then."

"Then what are we?"

I shrug again. "Why label it? Labels just make things complicated, after all."

She takes a deep breath and looks down at her hands. "Okay, well, since we aren't friends, I need to confess to you I lied. Craig and I...we didn't divorce because I didn't want children—quite the opposite. Abbey, I learnt I was a carrier of the gene: the Alzheimer's gene. Just like my mother and my grandmother. I never told him because I knew he would convince me, one way or another, that our baby would be fine. Thing is, there wasn't testing like there is now, and the risk, it wasn't one I was willing to take."

"June—"

"Please, Abbey...don't. I just needed you to know the truth. The diagnosis isn't new to me. I've been reminded of it since the day I walked out of his life, and it's part of the reason why I never found another. Most people want families, someone to love and fill a purpose in their life. Why start something you can't finish?"

The more we hold on to our memories, the wider the door to our past swings open— which more often than not is a curse—at least that's what my father believed. As I watch June speak about Craig, I notice the way her face softened and her smile grew wider with each passing moment. She's under that curse; even if she didn't realise it. June, despite two decades passing, is still in love with him. It's more evident than the rows of cars lined up next to us and the smell of the sea breeze waffling through the car's vents.

"Don't you think he deserves to know? I know I would..."

"It was the right decision at the time; it was also the wrong decision. The question of whether I would do the same or if I'd do it differently isn't one I've found the answer to. What I do know is the confusion of my decision still lingers in my mind, but I've come to terms with the fact that I'll never have all the answers."

"But what if—"

"But what if what?" she says, placing my hand over mine. "If he wanted to find me, Abbey, all he would've had to do is look."

CHAPTER SIXTEEN

JUNE - PAST

How do you know you're making the right choice? There's no guidebook to life. No way of knowing if the decision you make now won't one day haunt you for years to come. Every minute and every second counts, no matter how insignificant at the time it feels.

The day I decided to leave, it was raining, and they'd forecasted a storm would be making landfall come morning. Craig's flight wasn't due to arrive until five, so I booked myself on the early afternoon ferry, knowing there'd be a channel of water between us by the time he read my letter. I never expected fate would work against me.

First, the ferry had broken down, and a replacement was running late, and then Craig, for the first time in over five years, had finished work early. I knew it was him the minute I saw the flash of a yellow jacket weaving in between the cars.

"June!" I heard him calling, and I dropped into my seat, hoping he'd think the car was empty. It didn't work, and moments later, I heard him tapping on the window.

"Can we talk?"

"We have nothing to talk about."

"We have nothing to talk about?" he repeated, his voice breaking. "Are you kidding me? June, what the fuck is this?" He slaps the letter to the windscreen, and I can't look. I know exactly what the letter says, word for word; all the lies and half-truths that fill the pages were written by my hand, after all.

It took me two weeks to get the story right. It would've been easy to tell him there was another, but I knew Craig would never believe it. Instead, I told him I wasn't in love with him anymore and hadn't been for quite some time. I faked sentences of how I'd stayed, hoping it would get better, and weaved deceit into how if I stayed, we'd both be miserable. Then, with tears streaming down my cheeks, I wrote the fatal blow, telling him how the birth control hadn't been because I didn't want children; I just didn't want them with him.

"I don't believe any of it," he continued. "I know you, June. Most days, I know you better than you know yourself. What you are saying, I know it's all lies. I...just want to know why."

I closed my eyes, the tears coming hard and fast. "It's over, Craig. Believe what you want."

"No. It is not over. People don't look at each other the way we do if they no longer love each other. If you really mean it, say it," he said, slamming the window with his fist. "Tell me right here you don't love me anymore."

I shook my head; he knew I couldn't say it. I'd always been a transparent liar, and he was the one person in the world who could read me like I was his native language.

"That's what I thought," he said, reaching for the handle. "Let me in."

"I'm not letting you in."

"Let me in...please..."

"Go home."

"I'm not going home. Without you, that house isn't my home. Please...just let's sit and talk for a while. If you still want to go, I'll allow it. I...I just want to talk." He tried the handle again, and I could hear in his voice he was crying. "You're not leaving. Not like this."

Suddenly, the cars all turned their lights on, and Craig lost all composure. He knew he was seconds away from losing me and was desperate to stop that from happening, so he frantically tried the handle once more. "After spending a third of our life together, is this really how little I mean to you? You're what, June...you're going to drive onto that ferry and pretend I don't exist? Why? What did I do to deserve that?"

I tried to wipe my face, but the tears were coming too fast. "Craig, let me go."

"Why can't you look at me? Look at me, June, and tell me this is what you want!"

"I can't!" I screamed. "It isn't what I want; it's just what I have to do."

I could feel all eyes on us, watching the tragic end to a once-beautiful story. The boy who loved a girl with every inch of his soul, and the girl who loved a boy more than he'd ever know, who wanted him to have the chance at a life she couldn't give.

Slowly, the car in front of me started moving, and Craig stepped aside. I tried not to but couldn't help myself from glancing in the rear-vision mirror as I drove away. He didn't move, and around him, the rain seemed to fall in slow motion. Then I saw it, the way his face changed as inside, his heart broke into a thousand pieces, and the life he thought he'd have incinerated in seconds. I'd broken him. The one person in this life I never wanted to hurt, I'd destroyed, and as the dock disappeared from view behind me, a piece of me died with it.

CHAPTER SEVENTEEN

JUNE - PRESENT

"I am so pleased you came," Nora says, squeezing me tightly. We haven't seen each other in five years, but I'm convinced she doesn't age, since unlike me, her face isn't full of deep canyons and patches of leathered skin. "How was your drive?"

"Long," Abbey interrupts, pulling our bags from the boot.

"Ignore her," I say. "She has the attitude of a toddler who missed their afternoon sleep."

Nora laughs. "I can tell."

We both watch as Abbey heads for the door.

"Do you want to show her to her room and I'll make us a cuppa?" I ask.

Nora waits until Abbey is out of audible range and lowers her voice. "About that...do you think she'll mind sharing with Flynn?"

"Who?"

"Flynn. He's Caoimhe's son. There are two beds in there, of course, and he's working at the pub on lates all weekend anyway. She won't see him much. Or you two could just take my bed, and I'll sleep in there with him."

"Is he the gay one?"

"Jesus, Mary, and Joseph—I wish," Nora says under her breath. "Half the town's daughters are infatuated with him. Elijah is the one who is gay. Got out of here the second he could so his father didn't follow him everywhere. Poor pet. The whole world knew he wasn't interested in women before he did. That's why Caoimhe isn't here. He's doing a big Broadway show over there, and she flew over. Flynn's...nice. Although he can be a bit of an eejit at times, he's a good lad—respectful. Is that a problem?"

"Not at all," I say, heading for the door. "Abbey needs to lighten up a little. This will be good for her."

Once inside, Abbey and I head up the stairs and hook a right into the spare bedroom, and I can tell Abbey sees it first: an unmade bed with a dirtied pair of jeans and white Calvin Kleins at its base. The room is small—smaller than I expected—and the beds are within touching distance from one another.

"Is this a joke?" she hisses at me.

"Ah, would ya stop," I say, glancing at the open door. "Look, it's just for the weekend. He works late, and you won't even know he's here."

"You never said there was a 'he' involved. You said, quote, 'We are staying with an old friend and her girlfriend.' There was no mention of a 'he' of any sort."

"Well, in all fairness, I didn't know there was a he until two minutes ago."

"Where are you sleeping?"

"In Nora's bed."

She widens her eyes. "With her?"

"G'way outta that, we've known each other since we were kids."

"I'm going to stay at a hotel."

"No, you aren't. Firstly, you won't find one around here. Secondly, he's a nice lad. You might make a friend."

"I don't need any friends, and certainly not the kind you're suggesting."

"I'm not suggesting anything," I say, placing my hands up in mock surrender. "Besides, he wouldn't even give you a second look."

"Gee, thanks."

"Not like that, Abbey. He doesn't like girls...at least, the last I heard he didn't. You're all so fluid these days; I can't keep up." A small lie, she'd either love or hate me for in good time.

She ponders my answer, staring at the bag. Suddenly, she sighs, "You know what, I kinda hate you right now for this, but I'm really shattered. But if he tries anything, June, I swear, you're giving me the title to your house."

"Deal," I say, extending my hand.

She looks me up and down, studying my hand for a brief moment before shaking it. "Deal."

Back downstairs, Nora is at the table, waiting. From a distance, she still carries the same grace and affluent aura about her she'd inherited from her mother, but up close, the scars of her husband's death still lingered. Like many people, death changed her. Five years ago, she'd lost her husband, Callum. In her words, she'd never love another man, and who could blame her? Callum turned out to be the biggest catch there was thanks to his unexpected teenage glow up from scrawny raven-haired menace ways. But he was also one of the good ones, a faithful husband and a kind man.

Spending an hour in the same room as them was like travelling through the Healy Pass—nauseating yet oddly beautiful. There would never be another like him so instead,

Nora found companionship in a retired journalist with a Labrador personality named Caoimhe.

Although many suspected it, to outsiders, they looked like two widowed women. Behind closed doors, sharing the same bed and stolen kisses away from prying eyes, they'd built something few in life ever find once let alone twice. And as happy as she was, sealed off from the world behind the walls of their oddly shaped cottage with its even odder bright yellow door, part of me pained for her. With both families deeply ingrained in their religious ways, she'd never be able to share what they both rightly should.

"How did it go?" she asks, watching me as I slide into the seat across from her.

"I told her the last I heard he was gay. She'll be fine."

"You what?" Nora burst out laughing.

"Once you get to know her, you'll see why. Maybe he will introduce her to some of his friends. She needs friends, and she also needs to get laid."

"She does, or you do?"

I shoot her a look. "It's been so long for me, I've lost all need for it. Abbey, on the other hand, she's young, and I think in part wants to live a little; she just doesn't know how."

"Oh, to be young again. How old is she?"

"Same as Flynn I believe."

"You don't want her getting involved with him. Nice lad and all, but he's a right chancer. If she was my daughter, I'd be telling her to stay wide and clear."

"She's pretty fierce that one," I say. "I'm sure she could handle him."

"You never told me how you two met."

"It's a long story."

"Well, just as well we have all night, then."

I pause, watching as she pours tea into both of our mugs. I'd confessed to Nora most of my secrets over the years, but for some reason, I hadn't told her about the alzheimer's diagnosis. It was easy to lie behind a screen and pretend my life wasn't falling apart. I could tell her the good and dilute the bad, never once questioning if she doubted my honesty. Now, face to face with her, I feel the curtains drawing. One way or another, she'd learn the truth, and as my one true friend in the world, she deserved it to come from me.

"I have something I need to tell you."

She breathes in and closes her eyes for a moment. "If it's about the Alzheimer's, I already know."

"You do?"

"I've known for months. June, you may not remember, but you called me, thinking I was your local takeaway store. I didn't know it was you, at least, not at first. When I said you had the wrong number, you apologised and mentioned the diagnosis. You said sometimes, you get the numbers confused, and it wouldn't happen again. But it did. It's happened six times since, and all I want to know is why you felt you couldn't tell me?"

She reaches across for my hand, squeezing it gently. "You've always been able to tell me anything. I...I've been so worried about you. I knew one day you'd come to me, and that I had to wait...I'd started to think I was wrong."

I stare down at our hands laced together and tears start to fall. Within seconds, they go from a trickle to a waterfall, and I can't breathe. Everything inside feels tight like I'm trying to squeeze myself through a quarter opened door, and before I know it, I've lost all filter.

"I'm so scared," I whisper, repeating it until the words bind as one and no longer make sense.

Nora stands and comes to my side. She pulls me into her chest, stroking my hair and cheek as I bury myself in her. "I'm here," she whispers. "I'm here."

The words seem so simple. We tell each other our support is endless and the tap never runs dry, and at the time, we believe it. Thing is, nothing is infinite. I love Nora and as with Craig, I wouldn't allow her to become part of something she never asked for, even if she wanted to. Long after I'm gone, I want her to remember me. Not the me Alzheimer's is hell-bent on tearing apart limb by limb, memory by memory.

"I'm going to die by choice, Nora, before it gets really bad."

For a while, she says nothing before the tremors of her grief rupture to the surface. "Is that really what you want?" she finally whispers.

"It is."

"Then I'll come with you."

"You can't."

"Why the hell not?"

"We both know, you can't make a silk purse out of a sow's ear. Besides, I'd never ask that of you."

"You're not asking me. I'm offering," she insists.

"No," I say, gently placing my hand over her arm still wrapped around me. "That's one thing I'd never let you do, and you know it."

CHAPTER EIGHTEEN

ABBEY - PRESENT

For the first time in months, I dream of Scott. We're sitting at our old hookup spot we used to park at to avoid prying eyes, watching the sea hit the breakwater and flashes of lightning sparking like match flares in the distance.

"I haven't seen you in a while," I say.

He glances across at me. "I thought I ought to stop visiting you."

"What if I didn't want you to?"

"Sometimes, what we want isn't good for us."

I want to ask him why. I want to scream at him for leaving me and plead for answers he can never give me. Death, I've come to realise, isn't like other wounds. We can plug the void, filling it with distractions and self-forgiveness, but it still bleeds. His absence continues to bleed into all I am and all I lost as a consequence—that's something no amount of time will ever heal.

"Do you ever think about me?" I ask, watching as he walks to the water's edge. "Do you ever think about what would've happened if you'd stayed?"

He shakes his head. "I couldn't have stayed. It was never an option."

"What is that supposed to mean?"

"Either way, our life together was over." He lets out a deep breath, "What you did, Abbey, I...I could never have forgiven you for it. If you had stopped, just for one minute, and asked yourself if it was a good idea, she'd still be here." He pauses and runs a frustrated hand through his hair. "And maybe I would be, too."

"It was an accident, Scott. How...how can you even say that?"

He turns to face me, and I take him in. His face is changing the more time passes; it's as if my mind can no longer piece him back together. He looks like him, but there's something off, like I'm staring at a cheaply replicated copy, or the abstract of him has ripped, and I've tried to glue it back together.

"It wasn't an accident, and you know it. You hated me for what happened, and like a spiteful teenager, you wanted revenge."

"That isn't true."

"Isn't it, Abbey? Tell me then, what is the truth?"

Suddenly, before I can answer him, I'm jolted awake by a loud thud and find a guy on the floor next to me, trying to pull his pants off.

"Ah, Jaysus," he says, looking up at me.

"What are you doing?"

"Trying to get my pants off?" He grins. "You mind looking the other way? I'm a bit hammered, and I can't guarantee it'll be just my pants coming off at this rate."

I try not to look but can't help myself. Whatever I was expecting, it wasn't him. He's gorgeous, like the type of guy you'd see modelling activewear half-naked in a gym with a physique only unwavering discipline could create. Quickly, I shield my face and sink under the covers, listening as he struggles to get his pants off.

"Abbey, right?"

"That's right."

He must have managed to remove them, as I hear him fumbling around in the dark for his bed. "Nice to meet you."

"Can't say I feel the same," I mutter, sliding back under my covers. "What even is the time?"

"Like five?"

"Five am?" I groan.

"Yeah," he says with a shrug. "Maybe just closer to six now."

"And you've just finished work?"

He climbs into his bed. "I guess you could say that. Night, Abbey."

I let out a frustrated sigh. "Night."

Within seconds, he's fallen asleep, and I must have eventually drifted off, too, serenaded by the sounds of snoring and torrential rain. When I wake, sunlight is streaming through the window and the stranger is wrapped in a towel, pulling on a shirt.

"Morning," he says, without turning around.

"Are you really trying to make me feel awkward? Can you hurry up!"

"Calm down, would you. I was here first."

"What are you, ten?"

He laughs to himself. "What I am is hungry. Want to join me for breakfast? June and Nora probably won't be back till later, anyway."

"Wait...she's gone?"

"She left an hour ago." He turns to face me, frowning. "Her and Nora went out to get the messages. She came in here and spoke to you."

"The what?"

"Ah, I forget sometimes you ain't one of us—groceries—they went to get some food for tonight's dinner. But she said they'll probably be gone most of the day."

He phrases it like I should know what he's talking about, and I blink, trying to bring the memory into view. "I don't remember that."

"Happens to the best of us. I'll grab you a towel. Word of warning, the hot water is...temperamental. Be fast, and you should be fine."

Flynn isn't wrong. In the space of two minutes, the shower went from lukewarm to scorching hot, and by the time I've jumped out, half of me is covered in heat rash.

"Told you so," Flynn says, his eyes catching on my neckline as I walk down the stairs.

I glance up at him. He's changed into a knitted sweater and jeans with his hair falling loosely around his face. In the daylight, he's even more attractive than I first thought; it's almost a crime to women—to be that good looking and off-limits.

"Well, it's nice to see you have clothes on," I say, gesturing to him.

A smirk spreads across his face, and he turns to open the door. "When was the last time you took a ride?"

"Ride?" I stammer.

"Aye, on a bike," he calls back over his shoulder.

My cheeks flush, and I swallow the embarrassment of my lewd thoughts. "Uh...not since I was a kid."

I follow him outside where two rusty bicycles are propped up against the fence, and he wheels one over to me. The last time I rode a bike was college, and as I slide myself onto the seat, I can almost taste the pain I'll be in tomorrow.

"Try and keep as far to the left as possible," Flynn says as we head off. "The local peelers drive like they're doing laps at Mondello round here."

• • • •

THE IRISH COUNTRYSIDE has something truly majestic about it. From the rolling green pastures to the ancient stone walls and seaside shores, by the time we've reached the village I felt we've stepped onto a movie set. Flynn doesn't say much other than shouting directions back at me as we weave the streets, coming to a stop outside a small cafe which overlooks the bay.

Other than two women sharing a pot of tea in the morning sun, there isn't a soul to be seen, and we park our bikes up before heading inside.

"Take a seat," Flynn says, gesturing to an empty window table. "I'm just going to let Rosie know we're here."

He disappears behind the counter, and I watch as a young couple walk past with a newborn swaddled against the mother's chest. They are deep in conversation, holding hands with their steps in unison. I see people all the time, ones that remind me I'm still anchored to the ghost of my previous life. And yet, this one hits differently. Whether it's the lingering aftermath of my dream or the sombre undertones of fatigue pulling me under, my eyes start to water.

"I hope you don't mind a traditional break—" The sound of Flynn's voice breaks my thoughts, and he slides into the seat next to me, studying my face like a textbook. "Are you alright?"

"Why wouldn't I be?" I fire back.

"For starters, you look up to high doh."

"I'm just tired."

He studies me for a moment. "You're a terrible liar. You know that, right?"

I scowl. "How would you know if I was lying or not? We've known each other for five minutes."

He thinks about my answer. "It's your face. I look at it, and I feel everything you're feeling."

"Is that so? Okay then, tell me. What am I feeling right now?'

"Sadness. Pain. Regret." He pauses, staring deep into my eyes. "Loss."

"I'll take it June told you my life story."

"June told me many things, but that isn't one of them. I tell a lie, it isn't your face although, you do have a rather nice face. Actually, she told Nora, and I just overheard the conversations. I know all about how you're looking to bag yourself some luck with the Irish."

I cover my face. "She said that?"

"Yeah...I mean she pretty much tells Nora everything. Between you and me, Nora always plays her phone on speaker. I'm not sure if it's because she doesn't know how not to or because she is secretly going deaf but doesn't want the world to know."

"And you haven't told her, I take it?"

He grins. "Why would I? She's like the oracle here, guarding everyone's secrets."

"Hard to call them secrets if she isn't the only one hearing them," I say, folding my arms.

Suddenly, Flynn's face drops. I follow his gaze to a young woman approaching the desk. She's pretty, one of those easily enviable girls who are the complete package with an angelic face and body.

"Feck," he hisses, gripping my knees. "I...won't make it to the jacks, you'll have to hide me."

"How do you expect me to do that?"

"Your scarf. Give it to me."

I quickly unwrap my scarf and hand it to him. He wraps it around his neck and looks in my bag. "Got any sunnies, do you now, Abbey?"

"Oh my god, you're acting crazy. Here," I say, reaching into my bag and pulling out my oversized sunnies. He slides them on and rests his head against my shoulder, lifting a menu to disguise his face.

Even though I'm dubious of his plan, it seems to work. After talking to a plump woman behind the counter, the girl glances at me and smiles before leaving.

"Tell me when she's gone."

I wait, watching as the girl pulls out her phone and glances back at the cafe before she walks away. "You're safe. Now are you going to tell me what that was all about?"

He lets out a deep sigh and laughs, sitting up right. "Do you really want to know?"

I hit him across the head with the menu. "Actually, yeah, I do."

CHAPTER NINETEEN

JUNE - PRESENT

Nora asks me when I knew. Did it start the day I found out I, too, had the gene, or when did I notice things were going haywire? The more I ponder how best to answer her, the more elusive a concrete answer feels.

At the start, the signs were easily ignored or dismissed as tiredness or menopause-related hormonal shifts. It was little things like forgetting I was cooking and my gas alert metre triggering or leaving the refrigerator door open. Then I started writing lists, only to forget I'd written a list to begin with. It wasn't the day I found myself lost on the Thames bridle path or the day I couldn't find my way home. Alzheimer's had been making its presence known for years, and I'd pressed snooze over and over again till I couldn't anymore.

"It's hard to say," I admit, watching as she pours us a gin each. "If I'm honest, I feel there have been signs for years."

"June...if I'd known, I could've supported you."

I stare at her, trying to decipher the emotions behind her pained expression. There's something buried inside, something I know I've forgotten. Since I arrived, I'd seen it in her eyes, a conversation she wants to have but doesn't know how. But there's more—something deeper she keeps sidestepping.

"Are you hungry?"

She quickly passes me the glass and turns so I can't see her face.

"Nora...Did I...do something?"

I watch as she wipes her eyes without answering me.

"If I've forgotten something, I—"

"It's nothing," she interrupts, keeping her back to me.

My stomach drops as a sense of unease and dread hits me.

Where am I?

I pan my surroundings, and my eyes catch on a picture of two women caught in a romantic embrace. I fixate on their faces, trying to detect even the slightest familiarity, but I get nothing.

On bad days, my Alzheimer's is like a radio flickering in and out of signal. Some parts are clear, and there's no static or mismatched frequency. Others are fuzzy, broken, and full of looping white noise. Sometimes, it's just an hour or two out of the day, and then there are the days when all sense of clarity has been stripped away. My own handwriting appears foreign, my bed feels like a stranger's, and my home becomes a maze of four walls. I used to think it was relevant to my levels of stress and fatigue, just what each day would bring. Now, I feel I've fallen into a wheel spun by another's hand, dictating who's driving.

"What is it?" one of the pictured women says, turning around.

"I...I..."

"June?"

"I'm sorry. I..."

I try not to panic and sit patiently with my thoughts. If I can untangle just one knot, maybe the rest will come to me. Suddenly, it becomes too much, and I stand, sending my glass flying. It falls to the floor, shattering into a million pieces, and panic swells in my throat.

"June?" she says again, this time more concerned. "It's me—Nora."

"I...Nora? I'm sorry. I...I don't know who you are." I pace, panning the walls in a catatonic state.

"My name is Nora. We grew up together. Do you remember my mother, Dianne?"

"Dianne...Dianne..." I repeat, closing my eyes.

"We used to bike to school. Remember that? We'd always stop outside Mr Jones' house and pinch plums off his tree."

A memory of me picking plums with a short, olive-skinned girl with a bed of voluminous curly hair and pale green eyes comes into view. We're laughing, and it floods me with momentary comfort. I stop pacing and open my eyes again, catching on the woman's face. Her hair is no longer curly and is shorter than an inch, but those eyes, those familiar piercing eyes, are the same now as they were back then.

"Oh, god," I whisper. "Nora..."

"Hey, it's okay."

"No, it's not." I exhale a deep breath, my heart still pounding heavily in my chest. "It's never going to be okay."

Later that afternoon, Nora and I take a drive to the village. Everything is as it was when I left all those years ago, even if the odd letterbox had changed colour. We drive past our old school and down to the cliff faces, past Craig's old family home. It had sat vacant for years after; according to Nora, there had been a battle between the brothers over the estate.

"Have you seen him recently?"

"Who, Craig?" Nora asks, her voice growing hesitant. "Not in the last year. Have you?"

"I haven't seen him since the day we broke up."

"You're kidding me?"

"Well, I guess I live in London, so there was little chance of me running into him. How was he the last time you spoke?"

"Honestly, not great. He's had a hard life with his sister's battle with sobriety and having to look after those children. He never remarried, and the last I heard, he was still running his father's farm. Must be getting hard for him. We aren't exactly getting any younger."

To my surprise, I admit I think about him more than I'd cared to admit.

Nora glances at me. "You should go and see him. While you're here."

"Now, why would I do that?"

She shrugs. "I don't know. I just thought you might've wanted to."

"What I want is to spend time with you. After all, I don't have much time left. I've already set the date."

"Does Abbey know?"

I shake my head. "No, and she doesn't need to."

"You have to tell her."

"I can't. She'll try to stop me. I know she will."

Nora flicks on her indicator without answering me. Her lip is curled, and she's gripping the wheel so tight her fingers have blanched white.

"What is it?" I press, but she raises a hand to stop me.

"I can't do this today," she says.

And I nod in agreement, unsure of precisely what I am agreeing to.

CHAPTER TWENTY

ABBEY - PRESENT

By the time Flynn and I have stopped talking, the sun is getting lower in the sky, and I've missed three calls from June. Turns out the girl was Flynn's ex, and whilst they originally split amicably, the moment she found out he'd started seeing other people, a switch turned on inside her, turning into his worst enemy.

"Why are girls like...crazy?" He pauses, sipping his drink. "Actually, I take that back. You don't seem crazy."

"I am. In a different way."

"How so?"

"Em, my ex, I still have dreams about him."

"What dreams are we talking about here?" he says, raising his brow.

"Gross. Really?"

"I wouldn't judge you if you did."

"Why is the world so...obsessed with that stuff? It's been over a year for me, and I don't even think about it anymore."

"Not at all?"

I shake my head. "Not at all."

"Maybe you are an asexual type?"

"No, because when Scott was alive, I couldn't get enough."

"Maybe you just haven't met the right person to form that emotional connection with. Not everyone can do the one-night stand thing, and there's actually nothing wrong with that."

"But you do...the one-night stand thing."

He shrugs. "Yeah. Sometimes."

"How does that even work?"

"You go to their place or bring them back to your place and have sex. It's that simple."

"Do you like...text or have contact afterwards?"

"If you want round two, then yeah, sure. Nine times out of ten, it's a one-hit wonder."

"That is revolting."

He laughs. "What do ya know, Abbey is a wee prude."

"I am not."

"You just said sex is revolting."

"I said sex with strangers is revolting."

"Tell me something, have you even had sex with a stranger?"

"No. Of course, I haven't."

"Well then, Miss Abbey, best not knock it till you try it."

"I really don't see the appeal in sharing...all your germs and bodily fluids with someone you'll never see again."

He nearly loses his drink. "Tell me you did not just say that."

"It's true. Tell me I'm wrong."

"Aye, you aren't wrong," he says, trying to hold back laughter. "Are all English girls like you?"

"You make it sound like being me is a bad thing."

"Quite the opposite, Miss Abbey. I like you. You're a sound one you are."

We fall into silence, and I'm distracted by an older couple walking into the bar hand in hand. The world is like a multi-layered painting that reveals more details the longer you stare at it. And the second they walk in, I already know what they're about to order.

"It must be hard for you...coming back after losing everything," Flynn says, noticing my lingering gaze.

"Do we ever come back from something like that?" I draw a circle in the condensation on my glass, averting my gaze. "I'm starting to think I won't."

"Was June your therapist? Is that how you met?"

"No. I...I met June walking home. She lost her bus pass, so I paid for her fare."

"Stall it there." He studies me for a moment. "I ain't believing it. For starters, I've known June most of my life and she'd walk before she took money from anyone. Secondly, she told me you were her neighbour."

"What if I told you she was going to jump off a bridge into rush hour traffic? Does that sound like her?"

"Aye, you're right, it don't. But then again, Abbey, neither does driving nine hours to spend the weekend with a woman who you claimed you hated."

"What are you talking about?"

"June and Nora aren't friends. They haven't been for years. Maybe the dementia made her forget, or she wants to pretend she doesn't remember. Up until six months ago, they hadn't spoken in over a decade."

"Why? What happened?"

"I don't really know the full story, but I think it was about Nora's mother. June was treating her as a patient, and out of nowhere, Nora's mother decided she was going to take herself to Switzerland. They have these assisted dying clinics there, and June helped her forge the paperwork to present as a terminally ill patient. She wasn't sick, Abbey; she was mourning the sudden loss of her husband. She just needed time, but June convinced her otherwise."

I down the last of my glass, pondering his admission. It was easy to forget I don't really know June. This last week, she'd slotted into my life like she had always been there, and we act like we've spent years weaving in and out of each other's stories. Thing is, I don't know her story. I know a fraction of it, a sentence in a final chapter when the novel has already been written.

Flynn looks past my shoulder and sighs. "She's a good person, Abbey, don't get me wrong. That's the one reason I stayed in contact with her over the years. I just...I worry about Nora. You can forgive, or at least tell yourself you have? But you never forget. Unless you're June, and you can forget everything while the others have to live with the aftermath."

His comment may have been offhanded, but it annoys me. None of this was June's fault, and even if she couldn't remember, it wasn't as if she chose this. She didn't come across as the type to act without reason, so maybe, regardless of what Flynn and Nora believe of the situation, in her own way, she thought she was doing the right thing.

When we return to the house, Nora and June are talking in the kitchen. Instead of joining them, I head straight up the stairs. I'm conflicted; my mind feeling like it's stuck in a spin cycle, and the last thing I feel like doing is talking. A short while later, when I'm in the middle of sending a text message to Levi about what I'd learnt, I'm disrupted by a knock on the door.

"Everything alright?" Expecting June, I'm surprised when I glance up and see Nora instead. "She's worse than I expected," she continues, walking in and closing the door behind her. "I think I should take it from here, Abbey. She needs to go into a home."

I place my phone down. "It isn't what she wants."

"Do you honestly think she knows what she wants?" She takes a seat opposite me. "Abbey...she...she forgot where we were a half-dozen times today."

"She's also tired," I say, crossing my arms. "Michael said it could make her symptoms worse."

"Michael?"

"Her doctor. I appreciate your concern, but I'm handling it."

Nora scowls. "Handling it? If you were handling it, she wouldn't even be here."

"Her being here is your own doing. If what Flynn said is true and you hate each other, why is she here? Why text her back? Why allow her to come here and embarrass herself? Or is it just some game to you, revenge for what she did to your mother."

She doesn't answer me, and from the look in her eyes, I know I've hit a nerve.

"You know what, I'm done," I continue, standing. "I'm taking her home tomorrow. She doesn't need people laughing behind her back or making decisions for her."

I push past her and head down the stairs. Outside, it has started to rain, but I don't care. Pushing off on the bicycle, I head out into the darkness, hearing Nora shout at me from the porch about how I know nothing about June at all.

Perhaps she's right.

CHAPTER TWENTY-ONE

JUNE - PRESENT

After spending the afternoon driving yesterday, I'm exhausted by the time we get back. I excuse myself for a nap when, in reality, all I want is to be alone. I'd come here with such a purpose, and now my reasons for doing so evade me. It would be easy to dismiss it as a last hurrah before I fly to Switzerland and fill my decaying thoughts with the nostalgic memories of the last happy moments lived in my otherwise melancholic life. And yet there is a sense growing inside me that if I ran with that notion, I would be lying.

Staring at the ceiling, my thoughts drift to Craig. In the space of fifteen minutes, Nora had confessed more about Craig's life than I had gathered, periodically peering at his social media for the past decade. If what she says is true, and he'd lived his life alone, what good had my decision served? He'd never had the children I hoped he would, and going by what Nora said, like me, he had shut himself away from the world. My choice, one I thought I'd made for the better, could have, in reality, been a blessing disguised as a lifelong curse.

"What are you doing here? I told you I'd call you," I hear Nora's voice from downstairs, and I sit upright. Without the hum of gridlocked traffic and monotonous city noise, I can hear her as if she's standing right outside.

"I need to see her." I hear a male's voice say.

There's a pause, and I hear footsteps trail towards the kitchen.

"I don't think that is wise. She doesn't even know what year it is. One minute, she's here; one minute, she isn't."

The sound of the backdoor opening interrupts the quiet, and soon after, the voices muffle as they trail off outside.

"Of course, it isn't," Nora says, her voice dripping in disgust.

"Then what is it you want? Because I can't work that out."

"I want what's best for her and letting her do what she is thinking, that isn't it."

"So, locking her in a home until she has no ounce of dignity left is?"

The voices come back inside again, growing louder as the footsteps walk towards the lounge right beneath me.

"You're starting to sound like her."

"Well, maybe she was right about it all along."

"None of this is right," the male voice says in a raised tone. "I need to get going, but this...this conversation, Nora, isn't over."

Suddenly, I hear fast footsteps followed by the front door slamming. I stand to see whose voice it was, but when I reach the window, I can't see anything other than a plume of smoke as a car drives hastily away.

I must have drifted off as when I wake, it's dark, and I can smell cooking downstairs. I blink myself awake and realise I'm still fully clothed before checking the time. It's nearly six in the evening.

How long have I been here?

I lie there, sinking my head into the pillow, listening to a gentle wind rustling outside and trying to piece together the day's events. It's impossible. Whilst I know where I am and our venture into the village this morning, I've lost all sense of where the afternoon has taken me and the conversations that have taken place. And it's nothing short of terrifying.

I make my way downstairs and find Nora peeling potatoes over the sink.

"You must have been tired," she says, glancing at me as I walk into the room.

"Sorry. I get like that these days."

"No apologies needed. Drink?"

I shake my head and sit down at the dining room table. "I better not."

She watches me as I take a seat. "Have you heard from Abbey? I texted Flynn but haven't heard back."

"No, I haven't." My mind races as I try to remember where Abbey had gone, but I hesitate to ask for fear of sounding forgetful.

There's a quiet pause before she says, "They must be having fun."

I nod, my head starting to swim with the echoes of voices still ringing in my head.

Did the conversations of earlier really happen? Who was Nora talking to?

I want to ask, but at the same time, I'm scared that if I do, I won't like the answer. Instead, I swing the conversation back to Craig, wondering if he was the anonymous visitor.

"You said you haven't seen Craig in years, right?" I say slowly, trying to claw back the memory of all we'd discussed earlier.

"That's right," Nora answers without looking up.

"We were such good friends once. What happened?"

She dismisses my question with a shake of her head. "I feel like these are questions you should be asking him, June. I don't really know what happened to you other than what you told me."

"I'm asking you what happened to the friendship between us all, not what happened to me and him."

Nora sighs, pouring the peeled potato scraps into a bucket. "Well...I guess he blamed us for what happened. He came here for months, wanting your forwarding address, and I kept my word to you and didn't give it to him. He didn't just hate you for it;, he resented me as he considered me to be on your side and not his."

"And that's it? You never really spoke to him again?"

"We got busy. Life, it doesn't stop for anyone. Things changed. He was the only singleton left in our group, and you know, we tried to invite him places, but everything was different. He was different."

The sound of footsteps outside pulls both of our attention.

"Looks like Abbey and Flynn are back," Nora quickly says, placing the potatoes into the oven. Moments later, Flynn walks into the kitchen without Abbey.

"Where's Abbey?" Nora asks.

Flynn looks across at me, then back to Nora. "I thought she was with you? I've been at work. I'm just coming back for my bike."

"Shit," she says under her breath. "Abbey's got it. We got into a disagreement."

"About what?"

"It doesn't matter."

"Yes, it matters," Flynn says, trying to keep his voice calm. "I'm going to go find her."

He disappears out the door, leaving us in a tense silence, and I'm left staring at Nora, feeling a mix of conflicting emotions, questioning if it's a friend I'm looking at or a foe.

CHAPTER TWENTY-TWO

ABBEY - PRESENT

"Why do you look like you swam here?"

I'm seated at the bar when a man takes a seat next to me. After sitting on my own for the past hour, he's the first to admit his own intrigue as to why there's a pool of water beneath my stool and my clothes have stuck to me like paper mâché.

"I got caught in the rain," I say, taking another sip of my pint.

He signals to the bartender and slides off his jacket. "At least take my jacket so every man within a two-mile radius stops staring at your chest."

I glance down. My white cotton shirt has become invisible, exposing one of the bras June had purchased for me days prior. I'd been too caught up in my own turmoil to even notice, and a sudden wave of warmth floods my cheeks.

"What's your name?" the man asks, draping his jacket over my shoulders.

"Abbey. Yours?"

"Niall."

I look up. "Are you friends with Flynn?"

He laughs. "I guess you could say that. Is he why you're in such a mess?"

"Yes...no...not exactly."

"What's he done now?"

"Nothing other than make me realise how impulsive I am. I met this woman with dementia, and I barely know her but agreed to come here with her because she worries me. Now, I'm thinking I know actually nothing about her and who I think she is, isn't it." I pause, taking another sip of my drink, "We're staying with Flynn and Nora."

"Sounds—"

"Messy?"

"Complicated? It also sounds like you could use another drink. What are you drinking?"

I shrug. "I actually have no idea."

He reaches for my glass and sniffs it. "Murphy's."

"How do you do that?"

"Practice," he replies, placing the glass down.

I study him for a moment. From his charcoal grey fisherman knit to his fitted jeans, he looks like he's stepped straight from a menswear catalogue for the sartorially minded.

"I take it you're from the mainland," he continues.

"London."

"Thought so."

We settle into an easy conversation, and Niall tells me he was considering moving to Manchester in the spring after splitting up with his long-term girlfriend, who'd fallen for another.

"Here's to new beginnings," he says, raising his glass.

I laugh as our glasses clink together. "Here's to that."

After two more drinks, I feel more intoxicated than I've been in the past decade when Niall asks me if I'd like to dance.

"Oh, no," I say, shaking my head. "I really need to get going."

"How did I know that would be your answer?" He stands up. "Come on. Just one."

I shake my head again.

"Do you really need to get going?" he asks.

"I do." It's late, and I wanted to talk with June before she called it a night.

He stares at me for a few quiet seconds and then sits back in his chair. "How long are you here for?"

The question throws me. Part of me feels like June and me being here is a mistake, and the other half of me can't help but feel it's part of a reason I can't decipher. For the first time, I'm way out of my comfort zone, and it doesn't scare me the way I thought it would. As if, in a way, being around people who don't know the layers of my story is breathing life into a version of me who is longing to exist.

He leans forward and motions for me to come closer. I do, hesitantly, and he continues to lean toward me until his mouth is close to my ear. "I want to see you again before you go. Is that okay?"

I pull back gently, nodding. "I'd like that."

He smiles, and for a second, I wonder if he might go in for a kiss. I stand up hastily, causing the glasses to rattle in their place.

"I really need to go," I say, flustered, and before he gets the chance to say anything more, I leave.

I can't wipe the smile from my face as I start trailing back to the house. It's dark, pitch-black, and if it weren't for the luminance of the moon peeking through the clouds, I wouldn't be able to see a hand in front of me. After walking a half-mile, I see a silhouette of someone walking towards me, illuminated by the flicker of a headlamp. I soon realise it's Flynn.

"Stalking me, are you?" I yell at him, breaking out into laughter.

He casts me a disapproving look, and as he gets closer, I can see he's smiling. "Keep that up, and you'll wake up half the town."

"Do you mean...this?" I say, raising my voice.

"How hammered are ye, Abbey?" He pauses, dismounting from his bike. "And why do you have Niall Kelly's jacket?"

I can't answer him as a sudden surge of nausea spreads through me.

"Bleedin heck, tell me you aren't about to be—"

The bile rises in my throat, and before he can tell me to turn towards the grass, a projectile of vomit escapes, hitting the tarmac and splashing all over my legs.

"I'm not taking you home like this. June will have my head," Flynn finally says.

I wipe my mouth. "I'm not even that drunk."

"If you're not drunk, where's ma bike?"

As I open my mouth to apologise for leaving it at the bar, he cuts me off by wrapping an arm over my shoulder.

"Come on. We'll get some food for you, and then I'll take you home."

We U-turn back to the village, which seems to take half the time as it did on my own, and Flynn takes me out the back of the bar.

"I'm going to get you some water," Flynn says before disappearing back to the front.

I follow his path and see Niall has already long forgotten me and is chatting up a pretty redhead in a paper-thin body-con dress, and all at once, my naivete hits. I thought he was into me, and all he really wanted was to get between my legs.

Flynn enters again, the sound of water sloshing in a jug announcing his arrival, and hands me a glass of chilled water. "Here you go."

He follows my eyeline and lets out a sarcastic laugh. "Not jealous, are we?"

"Of course, I'm not," I say, taking the glass from him.

"He's a gobshite, Abbey. I wouldn't waste your time."

I shoot him a confused glare. "What?"

"That's his ex-wife." He walks into the freezer and returns with a scoop of chips. "He told us all how he'd never be in the same room as her again."

"That's his ex-wife? She's—"

"Hot—"

"Yes!"

He scowls. "No. Abbey, I mean chips. Hot...chips."

"I should really just shut up," I mutter, taking another sip of water to hide my embarrassment.

"No, on the contrary," Flynn says playfully, walking over to put the chips in the fryer, "Keep talking, Abbey. I want to know all your dark, drunk secrets."

After an hour of telling Flynn secrets I'd never reveal sober, like how I hate everyone at my workplace and how I secretly want to move to another country to rewrite my poor widow story, he decides I'm lucid enough to be dropped home. Once he borrows his co-worker's car, he drops me off without coming inside, and it isn't until I reach the stairs I realise June's on the porch. Sitting under a tartan blanket, smoking a cigarette with one hand and holding a glass of gin in the other, she eyes me suspiciously as I approach the stairs.

"I wondered where you got to, pet," she says, watching me as I struggle to remove my shoes.

"Is Nora still up?" I ask. "I owe her an apology."

"You don't owe me a thing."

I hear Nora's voice and look to the left of June, where I see her leaning up against the wall, disguised in the shadows.

"Do you want a drink?"

"I think I've drunk enough for the next year," I groan, walking up the stairs.

"Looks like it," June says, amused. "Whose jacket is that?"

Her question makes me laugh, and I steady myself against the wall. "In all honesty, I can't remember his name."

"Why don't you take a seat, and I'll get you some water?" Nora says, placing her hands on my shoulders. She guides me into the seat next to June, and I rest my head against her shoulders.

"Hey," June whispers as Nora disappears back inside.

"Hey," I murmur, closing my eyes in an effort to stop the world from spinning.

"How do you feel?"

I ponder her question, my thoughts filtering through me, but before I can answer her, a surge of nausea hits me again and erupts through my nose like a fizzing Cola bottle.

"Great. Just great."

CHAPTER TWENTY-THREE

ABBEY - PRESENT

I groan, feeling my head pounding as if I've run at full speed into a brick wall when I hear the door open. It's still dark, but I can make out Flynn's silhouette as he walks across to the wardrobe and removes his sweatshirt.

"Sorry, I didn't mean to wake you," he says without turning around.

"How was the rest of work?"

"Long. How was your date with Niall?"

"It was hardly a date."

He turns around, grinning. "He seems to think it was."

"It was one drink."

"One, huh? Why does it still smell like a brewery in here, then?"

I sink myself under the duvet and groan. "I'm never drinking again."

"Yes, you are. It's my birthday tomorrow, and you're coming. June and Nora are, too."

"I can still come and not drink."

"That's like going to the movies and not eating popcorn." He walks over and sits on his bed facing me. "Niall is going to be there."

"And that is even more reason not to drink. Tonight was bad enough."

"Not interested then, I take it?"

"You told me to steer clear of him!"

"You're right; I did. But I'm not your daddy now, am I?"

"What if I'm bad at it? Flirting, kissing, and all of that."

"That's impossible. It's easy. Stand up."

I give him a scrutinising look, attempting to gauge whether he's being sarcastic or not. "Excuse me?"

The warmth of my bed disappears as he stands and pulls back my duvet. "This will only take a moment."

"Hey," I protest, folding myself in half. "What are you doing?"

"Stand up, and I'll show you."

"Are you drunk?"

He considers my question. "A little. I had a few drinks at work."

Reluctantly, I get up, and the room starts spinning again. "You better make it quick. Because right now, there's two of you, and I...I really don't want to be sick again."

He laughs again and takes a step toward me. "You have to break the whole kissing strangers seal someday, might as well do it with me."

It takes a moment for his words to register. "You're joking—"

Before I can protest, his lips connect with mine. It feels awkward, at first, like my lips are fumbling for the right moves, but then it all falls into place effortlessly. There's an urgency in the way Flynn kisses me that I never experienced with Scott. His kisses are intense and fervent, as though he can't get enough. He moves me back, and I feel the softness of the bed behind me as he pushes me against it. We fall backwards, and both let out a shared, awkward laugh.

"Well...I mean...Wow..." I whisper, running a finger across my lips. "That...that wasn't so hard."

"I told you. Easy. You'll be fine."

He stares at me for a moment, his eyes focused on my lips, and then he leans in once more. This time, it's a completely different kiss than the one we just had. With both of his hands, he gently cradles my head and kisses me long, slow, and deep.

Inside, I can feel the safety wall crumbling. After a year of keeping my emotions in check, Flynn's kisses have opened a door to a world of feelings I thought I had lost. And whether it's the alcohol purging my senses away or a subconscious ripple of desire bubbling to the surface in the moment, I don't want Flynn to stop kissing me, and there's even a small part of me that wants more.

He wraps his arms around me, and I bury my face in his neck again. "I'm a bit drunk," I say.

His hands grip the nape of my neck, and he moves his mouth to my ear. "I know, which is why..." he says, kissing me gently on the forehead, then again on the tip of my nose. "I'm not going to sleep with you."

I feel a rush of conflicting emotions as he moves away from me, unsure if I'm disappointed or relieved by his sudden withdrawal. "Who said I would sleep with you even if you wanted to?"

He ignores my remark and stands, pulling back his covers. "You know," he says, adjusting his pillow. "You're not half as bad as you think."

I laugh, feeling the alcohol coursing through my veins, giving me a temporary boost of confidence. "On a scale out of ten, what am I? A two?"

He ponders my question, wearing a satisfied grin. "All things considered, I would give you a solid nine."

"Not a ten, then?"

"Don't take it personally," he says with a smirk. "Nobody has ever given me a ten."

The next morning when I wake up, Flynn is sitting at the end of his bed wrapped in nothing but a towel with a folded pair of jeans in his hands, and it all comes flooding back: the kiss, me vomiting all over June's shoes, and the argument with Nora.

I'm ready to dive into a full-on apology when Flynn glances at me, and I can tell something is wrong.

"What is it?" I stammer.

"It's June," he says slowly. "Don't panic, but she's missing."

I jolt upright and swing my legs to the side of the bed. "What do you mean she is missing?"

"She...must've left this morning. Her phone and purse are here. Nora left an hour ago to go look for her."

"No, no, no..." I whisper, standing. I walk over to the window and see June's car missing, and I start to pace, running my hands through my hair.

"Abbey, we'll find her."

"We need to go. Now!"

Although I have faith in June, I don't completely trust her to be by herself. Since we arrived, we haven't had a chance to speak one on one, so I'm not able to gauge how she's thinking or feeling.

Flynn raises his hand, and I look around for my jumper.

"Where the hell are my clothes," I yell, trying to sift through the mountain of Flynn's clothes blanketing mine.

"Here," he says, grabbing a hoodie from the foot of his bed. "It's clean...ish."

I don't hesitate to put it on. After all, a clean-ish hoody instead of a jacket that smells like fried chips and beer is the least of my concerns.

CHAPTER TWENTY-FOUR

ABBEY - PRESENT

Just as quick as my panic had set in, it dissolves as we hear the front door open and the sound of June and Nora's voices echoing from downstairs. Without thinking, I race down the stairs still wearing Flynn's hoody when I'm met with surprised faces by both her and Nora.

"Where was she?" I ask Nora.

"Having a drink at the local, no harm done."

"You had me worried," I say, sliding into the seat next to her.

"I thought we'd already established you need to worry less. Nice jersey, by the way."

My cheeks turn bright red with embarrassment, and I quickly glance at Flynn, who seems oblivious to my discomfort with his head buried in his phone. "It isn't what you think."

"I wouldn't blame you if you did. He's not bad looking. Although, he does have a reputation."

As if I couldn't be any more embarrassed, I feel my whole body ignite. "It really isn't—"

"Don't you know the saying, June," Flynn interrupts, sliding his phone back into his pocket. "Believe half of what you hear."

"When it comes to you, it's because I know you that I do believe everything I hear."

I can tell just from the glint in her eye she's already scheming, wondering if behind closed doors her plan had been a success. Suddenly, Nora clears her throat.

"Right, birthday boy, we need to get organised for this party. Do you know who's coming yet?"

"Only Callum can't make it. Everyone else should be there," he says, turning to face me with a pointed look. "Niall and the rugby lads, as well."

"Well," June says, her voice betraying her amusement. "Abbey might be able to return the jacket she stole to its rightful owner. How lovely."

I glare at both of them, and if looks could kill, they would've dropped dead right then and there.

After having an early dinner, we head down to the bar just shy of eight. Flynn had already left earlier, telling us he'd meet us there and, as we step inside, I can't help but feel everyone's eyes on me.

Nora, after disagreeing with three of my outfit changes, had me under her wing as her fashion protégé. Disgusted by my staple choice of jeans and a cardigan, she'd sifted through her closet and found a skintight black number with a daring thigh slit—much to my horror. And I'd agreed to wear it. Not because I wanted to but because June had said if I dressed my age for one night, she'd never ask of it again.

"My guests of honour," Flynn calls out, his eyes not leaving mine as we cross the room. Amidst the cheers and laughter of the crowd, June drags me to the bar and orders shots for the two of us.

"I think you have a secret admirer," she says, looking back at him.

I try to act unbothered by his gaze. "He's drunk."

"And so what if he is? Why is it so hard for you to believe people find you attractive, Abbey?"

Ignoring her, I downed my shot and shuddered at the taste, wiping my mouth clean. I'd never had much esteem for myself, and as I'd got older, it'd only become worse. Maybe that was the reason I hadn't tried dating. It wasn't because I lacked the experience or I didn't want to. Perhaps, above all else, I feared the risk of rejection and what that would do to my already dwindling self-worth.

"What did he do to you?" she continues, analysing my every move.

I stare down at my empty shot glass, the rim still littered with salt. "What did who do?"

"Scott."

Running my fingers through the salt crystals, I can't answer her, and my thoughts drift back to the moments before the crash happened. I'd collected Scott from the airport, and neither of us had spoken a word to one another. While I was lost in thought, replaying the scenes of him at the bar in my mind, he was absorbed in whatever was happening in his phone. Aila must have picked up on my unease, as she, for the first time in weeks, was silent.

"Is...is everything okay?" he finally said, sliding his phone into his pocket.

"Fine. Why wouldn't it be?"

He paused. "You just sound...short."

I bit my lip, holding back the hurricane of words desperate to escape. I felt like screaming about how I knew what he said and how I'd been getting less than two hours of sleep every night for the past two weeks. I wanted to confess I was worried about my thoughts lately and how three days ago I'd nearly left Aila at the supermarket in her car seat because, in my mind, anywhere but with me would be a better life for her. Everyone talked about all the love you feel for your child. Antenatal classes are full of promising discussions on how you'll find a purpose in life you never dreamt imaginable and midwives tell you bonding takes time. Thing is, the more sleep-deprived I'd become, the more I started to resent Aila and nobody, not one person, talked to me about what to do with those thoughts.

"I'm fine," I said.

"Talk to me."

Talk to him? And tell him what? How my body hurt and not just my nipples or the struggling to heal stitches between my legs, but everything right to the bone was crying, longing to escape the hands of the sleep deprivation wound tight around my neck. Did I say I'd began to hate him? As he drank and danced with half-naked strangers, I couldn't remember when I last had a shower or a meal without the sound of screaming around me. He got to dine out in fancy restaurants and wear nice suits, whereas all I'd eaten in three days was cold toast and lukewarm instant coffee. It was a form of self-inflicted punishment that I didn't expect to be facing alone. After all, Scott promised me that it wouldn't be the case. As it turned out he wasn't just a liar, but he broke promises, too.

"Abbey..." he continued, and I realised we'd been sitting in silence for too long.

"It's nothing."

"If it's about Aila, I'll take over when I get home–"

"It's not about her," I snapped.

"Then what is it about?"

I took a deep breath, glancing in the rear mirror. As soon as the words left my mouth, I wished I could take them back. "It's about us," I said, and the silence that followed was deafening. I waited for him to say something, anything, but he remained quiet. And that's when I knew it was over. Instead of asking what I was talking about or pushing for more details, he said nothing. Still, I held my breath and silently begged for them to come. An apology or even a proclamation on how we'd make it better, but all Scott gave me was the irreversible pain of silence.

"I could move out?" he finally said, and it was enough for the anger inside to breach.

"Are you fucking serious?"

"You just said—"

"I said we need to talk about us, and you're making it sound like I just asked for a divorce."

"And you wonder why I can't be around you for more than five fucking minutes," he says, hitting the dash. "You're insane. You're fucking insane."

We began to yell at each other, and Scott told me he doesn't even know who I am anymore. And maybe, in a way, I didn't either. The Abbey he'd so easily forgotten wanted a different life. She wanted adventure, love, and to live each and every day as if the promise of sunrise wasn't given. She used to find joy in simple things and her dreams felt more alive than reality. He may have forgotten her, but I hadn't. If anything, I grieved for her, convinced she was never coming back.

Aila started to stir. In less than a minute, she transitioned from whimpering to full-blown angry crying, causing me to lose my composure.

"I hate you," I screamed, breaking out into sobs. "I hate what you've done to me. To us!"

It sets Aila off more and her cries intensified to the point I felt them reverberating through my body. I knew I had to find a safe place to stop the car, so I scoured the road. There was no shoulder for at least another three miles, so I reached behind me and used my left arm to rock her seat the best I could. For a split second, I consider just driving us off the edge. It's one of those brief delusional thoughts without any substance, and yet it still scares me.

Suddenly, a flash of red caught my eye, and my heart raced when I realised I'd somehow drifted into the wrong lane.

"Shit," I yelled, trying to swerve. But it was too late. I was jolted forward as the car violently spun, and the sound of breaking glass filled my ears, drowning out everything else. Seconds later, it hit. It was another car from behind, and my head hit the dashboard at full speed.

I must've lost consciousness as I emerged from the darkness, only hearing the sound of muffled voices and hissing from the folded bonnet, the smell of gasoline suffocating the air.

"Aila," I whispered, blinking to gather my surroundings. I paused, listening for a soft whimper or a cry amongst the noise. There was nothing, and it would later go down as the loneliest moment in my life. I tried to move, but the scrunched metal had me in its vice. Behind me, the boot of the car had collapsed in on itself, folding like paper, and the fear started to set in. I couldn't see or hear her, let alone Scott.

"Can you hear me?" I heard a man's voice.

"Y...Yes...Yes, I can." I wiped between my legs and realised that the liquid pooling there was not urine or water but blood.

"Everything is going to be alright. Can you turn the car off?" It wasn't until he asked that I realised the car is revving, and I feel for the button to switch it off.

"Is it just you in the car?"

"No," I said, my voice breaking. "My..." I paused, "my partner...my baby...is...is she okay?"

I could hear the sound of metal being pulled back, and he let out a short gasp.

"My baby?" I said again. "Please tell me she's okay."

Despite my question, the man only offered the repeated statement that everything will be fine. It didn't take a fool to know he was avoiding the question, and I didn't blame him.

"Ambulances are on their way," I heard another man's voice say.

I waited, listening as the voices started talking but sounded as if they were drifting further away. My eyes drift to the passenger seat and I call out for Scott. Underneath a small gap in the metal, I can see a small patch of his jeans, but he doesn't answer me.

"There's a sole occupant deceased in that car and two injured in the Fiesta," the same man's voice continues. "How many are in the Golf?"

"One woman on the driver's side. Passenger, male mid-twenties deceased and a baby in the passenger rear," he paused, lowering his voice as if to shield me from hearing, "deceased."

I snap from my thoughts when we are interrupted by Flynn as he staggers to the bar. "And why do you both have faces like a slapped arse now?" he slurs, wrapping his arm around me.

I look across at June and then back over to Flynn. The air has become suffocating with the voices around me louder than Glastonbury. "I'm sorry," I say, pulling his hands from my shoulders. "I need to go."

"Abbey—"

I place my hand over June's, cutting her off. "You stay here. Nora would want you to. I think...I think I just need to be alone."

And with that, I get up and leave.

CHAPTER TWENTY-FIVE

ABBEY - PRESENT

I shiver as I step out of the bar, feeling the biting chill of the night air. After hooking a right, I start walking, and before I reach the corner, the sound of hurried footsteps echoes from behind me.

"Abbey," I hear Flynn say, "where are you going?"

I repeat that I need to be on my own when he pulls me to a stop, placing both hands on my shoulders.

"What happened? Did June say something?"

I shake my head, unable to look at him. "What could she possibly say? She barely knows me."

"Look at me."

I shake my head again.

"Abbey, come on. When you leave here, the chances of us crossing paths again are slim. You could tell me anything, and it wouldn't even matter." He pulls me off the road, and we take a seat on a stone wall. "What is it?"

"You should really get back to your party," I say, turning my head away from him.

"A party is only a party if everyone is having a good time."

I hold his gaze, transfixed by the silhouette of his lips in the dim light until we're both jolted by the sudden brightness of high beams approaching. The car slows down and pulls in front of us when I hear June's voice as the driver's side opens.

"Shouldn't you be entertaining your guests?"

"Should you even be driving?" Flynn shouts back playfully. "Whose car...Wait...is that my car?"

She doesn't answer him. "Come on, you two. Let's go for a drive."

"You're not—"

"You either go back to your party, birthday boy, or come with us. Your choice."

He looks at me and then back to her. "I really don't think you should be driving."

"I'm not driving," June says, opening the passenger door. "Abbey is."

I freeze, and it hits me what June is doing. She knows I haven't driven since the accident.

Reluctantly, Flynn heads for the rear passenger side and for a while, we all sit in the car, staring at the faint flicker of lights in the distance. Puffing on a cigarette, June tells me to take as much time as I need since neither of us is leaving the car until I've driven it at least five miles.

"I've had a shot of tequila," I protest. "What if I get pulled over?"

"A shot of tequila is hardly going to make you blow a DUI."

"Why are we even doing this? It's silly."

"It's far from silly, Abbey. I saw the way you looked in the bar. I'll be dammed if that dead fucker ruins the rest of your life."

She leans forward and switches on the radio, holding the cigarette between her lips. Seconds later, *Mr Brightside* blares from each speaker. "Put it in drive, and let's go."

For a while, I stare at the road, listening to June hum along to the lyrics with her feet pressed against the dash. It's dark and even though I can't see more than a mile ahead of me, I remember biking down it with Flynn without giving it much thought. Maybe June's right—I think too much.

Slowly, I reach for the ignition, turning it over.

"There we go," June says, nudging my shoulder. "Progress."

My laughter turns to tears.

"Don't cry."

"I'm not," I say, wiping my face. My eyes flick upward, and I find Flynn's gaze fixed on me in the rearview mirror, his brow furrowed as if he's trying to interpret the silent conversation happening between June and me. He'd been so quiet, I'd almost forgotten he was there. After taking a deep breath, I reach for the handbrake and release it before pressing the accelerator slowly. It jolts, at first, like we are in the midst of a first driving lesson before we set off.

I glance across at June, winding down her window. "You haven't told me where we are going?"

"Keep driving," she says. "I'll tell you where to go."

After doing a loop of the town centre, June takes me up a backroad before instructing me to pull into a grassed-over lookout spot.

"Leave the keys inside," she says, opening her door.

"Is...is that...safe?"

She pretends to debate the question, giving me a look as she walks in front of the car. Of course, it's safe. We are in the middle of nowhere, after all. I follow her and Flynn out, and we duck under a broken wire fence before taking a seat. For a while, none of us says anything, listening to the sound of the waves crashing beneath us when June reaches into her bag. To me, it looks like another cigarette when she places it to her lips, but Flynn is wiser about the world and bursts out laughing.

"Are ye trying to get us all arrested now?"

Suddenly, it hits me. "Is that weed?" I hiss, trying to fling it from her hands. "Are you crazy?"

She swats at my hand, turning her head away from me. "Don't tell me you've never been stoned before."

"Of course, I haven't."

"Well, we ought to change that."

"It's illegal."

"Only if they find out."

I look across at Flynn who is trying to hide the smirk on his face.

"Stop her. This isn't a good idea."

June lights up the end of the joint, and the pungent smell of weed fills the air as she takes a deep drag before passing it to Flynn. To my shock, he follows her lead.

"Go on, Abbey," Flynn says, grinning. "Have a laugh. Just once."

He holds it out for me, and I watch as the smoke spirals and dissolves into thin air. I'd always been a good girl. The one who sober drove her friends and achieved straight A's. Not once had I even been drawn to dabble in life's darker side, and yet now, it's all I want to do.

"Go on," June says encouragingly. "You're safe."

"We're sitting on the edge of a cliff, and you're telling me to get stoned. How is that safe?"

She doesn't answer me, and Flynn leans forward, inching closer.

Slowly, I take it from his hands and bring it to my lips. I take in too much smoke, and it sends me into a coughing fit.

"A little slower, Abbey." Flynn laughs. "Hold it in a little and let it do its magic."

I can feel him watching me as I take another drag before handing it back to him.

It passes around our half-circle three times, and then we all lie back in the grass, staring at the stars above us, listening to the sound of the waves crashing beneath us.

"There's something I need to tell you," she finally says. There's something wrong. Her voice is void of all her staple hard, sarcastic stone, and I can feel the tremors in each word. She starts by saying, "When we get home," and then proceeds to tell me about her decision to travel to Switzerland to die. "I don't expect you to come, but, Abbey, I would love it if you did."

I sit on her words, trying to digest their meaning as she continues on, telling me how she's been researching assisted dying and had found a clinic. I'm too stoned to fully comprehend the full meaning behind what she's saying, and as Flynn reaches it across for my hand, it starts to sink in.

"I forgot where I was again, three times today. Each time, it's getting worse. I...I can't even explain it. It's like...I feel one day...that'll be it. Instead of coming back, I'll be lost forever, and I don't want that."

"I don't...I don't want you to go," I whisper. "Not yet."

She looks across at me, her tears illuminating from the lights behind us. "I know. But you're going to be okay. I know that now."

"No, I'm not. I'm a mess."

"We're all a mess, Abbey. Some of us are just better at hiding it." She lets my hand go and reaches behind her for a piece of rock. "I used to park up here all the time when I was younger. When I wanted to let something go, I'd pick up a rock and yell out whatever was bothering me and throw it into the sea. You should try it."

I watch as she stands, walking to the edge. For a moment, she stares down at the rock before flinging it out to sea, screaming fuck Alzheimer's at the top of her lungs. Her voice echoes all around us, becoming at one with the hymn of the sea below. "Your turn," she says, turning to face Flynn and me.

Reaching behind me, I grab a rock and stand, walking over to her until we are side by side with our shoulders touching. While rubbing my thumb over the sharp, splintered edge of the rock, I confess under my breath, "I kissed Flynn." I'm not sure why it's the first thing that comes into my head, but it seems better than discussing June's alternative.

"Did you enjoy it?" she whispers back.

"I did."

"Will you do it again?"

Oblivious to how loud we are whispering, I tell her, "I wouldn't say no."

She stays silent for a long moment, glancing back at Flynn. "He is actually a sweet lad. I think a bit like you, he's just wanting to find his place in the world."

My gaze lowers, and I stare at the ground, pondering what to say next. Then it hits me, what I need to say. I turn back to the water, inhaling a deep breath, and fling the rock as hard as I can.

"Fuck Alzheimer's, and screw you, Scott."

CHAPTER TWENTY-SIX

JUNE - PRESENT

The next morning, I wake before everyone else and decide to take a drive. It's happening again, my mind has blurred the lines between fiction and reality. Last night, I'd woken several times to visitors at the foot of the bed. First, it was my mother, only this time, she was smiling. For a while, with the duvet tucked under my chin, I watched her. There was no panic or raking questions of logic; I just sat there, feeling nothing but a growing sense of comfort.

Then came my father. Twenty years my mother's senior, he died before I reached double digits in age. I know his face and stories of him from others, yet my memories of him are few and far between. It's a funny thing to grieve something you never really had. I've gone my whole life burdened with a sense of what if things had been different? And it's like Pandora's box. Once you open it, it never ends.

From pivotal moments in my life's successes to decisions I've had to make without a guiding hand, he's been along with me for each one of them, a void I could never quite replace.

By the time I reach the village, the morning sun has defrosted the fine layer of frozen film from the ground. The postman is loading his van, and a pair of gentlemen are heading down to the beach with their fishing rods. It's a different pace of life here. Unlike London, which runs off milliseconds and systemic bedlam, here, everything is as life should be but rarely is.

I keep driving up the hill and take a right onto Craig's road. The farm was one of the largest in the area. It spans both sides of the road to the fringe of the village on one side to the sea cliffs on the other. We'd always planned to take over when his father retired, but when I graduated from university in the city, I knew my heart would never be where Craig needed it to be. He was counting down the days until he could return, whereas I was counting down the days until I could convince him a flat in the city would make him just as happy.

As I rise over the hill, the farmhouse comes into view. Surrounded in morning fog and boxed in by ageing fir trees, its beauty, unlike life, remains unchanged. I pull over and stare at it for a while, hit by the swift onset of memories. Though I'm fast losing my present, the past has become more vivid than ever. In a way, it's the blessing stitched into the otherwise odious curse, allowing me to relive moments I thought had been lost in life's current forever.

The sound of a tractor pulls me from my daydream, and I glance up, seeing a man on a rusted Ferguson, getting out to open a gate in the paddock to my right. There's something in the way he moves which feels familiar, but he looks too old to be Craig. For a while, pretending I'm on a call, I watch him until he looks in my direction.

Shit.

I reach for the ignition, but it doesn't tick over. So, I try again. Nothing. It doesn't go unnoticed, and the man jumps the fence and makes his way over to me. As he gets closer, I know it's him, and I panic, fearing he'll know it's me. Quickly, I reach for my sunglasses before getting out.

"Morning," he says. "Everything alright?"

"I pulled over to take a call, and now I can't get her to start again."

"New technology, you can never rely on it." He places his hands on the bonnet, pulling it gently. "Do you mind unlocking it, and I'll take a look?"

I nod and open the door. I'd never opened the bonnet before, and as I search for the lock, I can feel my cheeks growing more flustered.

"It should be right under the wheel," he continues.

He's here. I could see him and hear him humming to himself, the sound materialising our memories like igniting a match. His appearance seemed to have altered since the last time he updated his profile picture. He'd always been borderline muscular, a genetic and laborious trait, but now he's lean and his broad shoulders are starting to slump. And while his hair had thinned and turned a dark shade of grey, it had the same effortlessly tousled look I'd always adored.

After I'm still unable to find it, he walks to the driver's side and peers in.

He laughs and points. "Well, I think I've found your problem. You're still in neutral."

I follow his gaze, feeling my nerves climbing.

There are so many things I want right now. I want to wrap my arms around him and feel his lips against mine. I want to confess to him all the things I've kept bottled up over the years, but most of all, I want to tell him the truth. But when our eyes catch, he doesn't look at me like a woman he once loved or even someone from a past life he knew. The way he looks at me is like a complete stranger, and I resist my own screaming desire in the belief that maybe keeping it that way is morally the right thing to do.

"Thank you," I choke, pressing the button again. This time it starts without hesitation, and the silence between us is filled by "Blower's Daughter" by Damien Rice playing on the radio.

"Good song," he finally says, his eyes not leaving mine.

To an outsider, the song is just a song, one that has been played and will continue to be played a million times. To us, it's the song we first danced to as husband and wife and the source of countless memories no other would ever know.

"I do love me a bit of Damien."

"Sorry, I didn't catch your name?"

I swallow and blurt out the first name that comes to mind. "Abbey."

"Nice to meet you, Abbey," he says. "You have yourself a good day now."

"You, too," I reply quietly, and with that, he turns and walks away.

Driving back to the house, overcome with emotions, I lose sense of where I am. All of the landmarks and familiar sights I'd registered to myself have dissolved, and as I pull into a lookout overlooking the cliffs, the tears start again.

I could count on one hand the number of times before coming here that I'd cried. And yet, surrounded by a life I could've had and all I gave away, it feels like it's all my eyes want to do. Grief and guilt are the two hardest emotions most of us will experience in this life, and I was a fool to believe them to be mutually exclusive. They aren't. They can exist in perfect harmony, one step in line with the other, and it doesn't matter if it's been a decade or a year, if you pretend they don't exist, it's only a matter of time till it finds you.

The minutes pass into an hour, and I feel frozen, unable to move when a car pulls into the car park next to me. I hear the crunch of gravel as whoever was inside approaches, but they stop short of reaching me.

"June," I hear a male's voice say.

I turn, and my eyes land on Craig. There's no need for words. We understand everything we are not saying. He keeps walking until we are within arm's reach of one another.

"How did you know?" I whisper.

"Abbey? Is that really the best name you could think of?"

I laugh, wiping my eyes. "I thought it might've been the ironic timing of the song."

"That, too, and the fact you can't get cellular reception on my road."

I laugh again, and slowly, he takes another step forward before wrapping his arms around me. It's enough to unravel the coil binding my composure completely. I start crying without restraint, fisting the chest of his jacket with my body shaking in such violence that I can hear the gravel beneath us shift under our shoes.

CHAPTER TWENTY-SEVEN

JUNE - PRESENT

"Do you know I must've sat in this exact spot a hundred times over the years," Craig says as we climb through the safety fence and take a seat, resting our backs against its steel frame.

I follow his gaze, watching the waves below us crash against the rocks. We'd always come here to escape the world, whether it was Craig's religious parents or my mother's eye, and now, two decades later, in a bittersweet turn of events, it was no longer the world we were trying to evade, it was the past.

"I wanted to call." As I speak, my voice trembles and I clamp my lips together, biting down hard. "Not a day went by where I didn't want to pick up that phone, Craig. I...I made a mistake."

He looks down, shaking his head. "It wasn't a mistake. A mistake is saying the wrong thing, then apologising later, or drinking a little too much and making yourself look like a fool. This was a choice, June. One you made, and I was just expected to live with."

"I couldn't be what you wanted. I thought I was doing the right thing."

"You couldn't be what I wanted? How would you even know what I wanted if you never asked?" He reaches for my hand and turns it over, staring at how perfectly it seems to fit into his. "I don't want to argue...since you called—"

"Hold on. Called? We haven't spoken in over two decades."

"June, you've been calling me every day for the last year. Always at ten minutes past five, never a moment later, like you used to when we were married. It's like a loop. You tell me you're running a bit late from the office and will be home soon. Lately, it stopped, and I was worried you'd...you know...gone."

With a sudden crystallising thought came the first stirrings of rising panic. I rake through my mind, hoping but failing to find any trace of the conversation buried within the caverns. "Is that all I'd say?"

"No," he says, his voice reducing to a whisper. "Some days, we'd talk as if, in your mind, time had stood still. You'd ask me what I wanted for my birthday, and I'd pretend because I was worried that if I didn't, you'd stop calling, and I'd lose you again."

What was he talking about? Forgetting names, faces, and the infamous soda bread recipe my mother gifted me was understandable. This, I couldn't understand. If what Craig and Nora are saying is true, and I've been living a double life, what version of my story is fiction? The one where the woman, in the space of a year, had gone from living a relatively conscious life in control and self-aware or the one where I had calculatedly painted an imitation of such when, in reality, nothing could be further from the truth.

I pull my hand back. "I need...I need to go."

Craig doesn't move as I stand and climb back over the fence. He still remains unmoved as I cross the car park. Just as I'm reaching for my keys, I hear the sound of his footsteps behind me.

"Why did you come back?"

I close my eyes. Deep down, there had to be a reason, and yet, wherever it was, I can't find it. Was it because I wanted forgiveness? Was it because before I die, I wanted to flood the last remaining morsels of consciousness with memories I'd longed my whole life to create? Or was it a more selfish and egotistical reason? I wanted to control the narrative of how our story ends.

"Do you know how hard it was for me to accept you'd gone?" he continues. "In some ways, it was like you'd died, June. You just vanished. And I tried...I tried to move on, and I couldn't. There was always something unfinished between us, and no matter how hard I tried, it was there. Right there, reminding me you had a piece of me no other could."

His footsteps slow, and I turn around to face him. I let out a slow breath and meet his eyes.

"I came to say goodbye. In a week's time, I'm going to Switzerland. This life, it's no life. I wake up, and I have to remind myself what day it is. My reflection...I'm starting to forget it. I can't cook anymore without risking setting my house on fire, and all these conversations you say you've had with me, Craig, I can't remember a single one of them."

"You don't have to do this. Please...please don't do this."

As he reaches out for me, I instinctively take a step back. "I have to."

"No...June, you don't," he says, his voice beginning to tremble. "You have a choice. I could look after you. We all could."

I know he means it. Of all the things Craig is, sincere is the backbone. But what good would it serve if I slowly lose myself and the beauty of our memories disintegrates?

"It isn't what I want."

Craig's demeanour changes, and his stare goes from admiration to one of hurt. "Do you even know what you want? Or is it just something else you've forgotten?"

"That's not fair."

"No, what's not fair is, once again, you're not giving me a choice. I've known you my whole life, June, since we were kids. What you're thinking...What you're proposing...it isn't you."

I stare at him, and it all comes flooding back. The evenings where we would lie by the creek discussing our dreams, our first kiss on the dancefloor at the tavern. Nights where we would stumble home drunk, waking up the village, singing at the top of our lungs. University parties where in a crowded room, I only had eyes for him, and the feeling of loving him was so much, at times, it felt as if it could suffocate me. We weren't kids anymore, and the fire that once burned had reduced to embers, but in a world growing more foreign by the day, Craig was and always would be the one place that felt truly home.

"The me you think exists no longer does," I say, wrestling back my emotions before turning to face the car. I wait, pausing as my hands wrap around the handle, expecting him to continue, only he doesn't. Slowly his footsteps retreat, and I know it's over. Craig fought for me once, and all it did was bury him in a hole that life didn't give him the tools to fill.

"My mistake," he says under his breath. "Seems I know more about you than you do these days."

He wasn't about to do it again, and who could blame him for that?

CHAPTER TWENTY-EIGHT

ABBEY - PRESENT

I wake up to the creak of the bedroom door opening and the sound of Flynn opening the wardrobe door. Once I've blinked myself awake, I can see he's fully dressed, sliding on a puffer jacket.

"Morning," he says without turning around.

"Do you have work?"

"Not today." He pulls up the zip and faces me. "June's missing again."

I feel like I've been walking through the desert for hours, my mouth dry and my head pounding, but his words sober me instantly.

"What do you mean she's missing?"

"Nora, she got a text from Rosie at the bar this morning checking in on her. Apparently, she saw her driving from the direction of Craig's house."

"Craig...as in...Craig...June's Craig."

A flicker of amusement spreads across his face. "Yes, Abbey. Craig...Craig."

"How would she even know where to find him?"

"Why wouldn't she? He's lived in the same house since the day she left."

He looks at me and he breathes in and then breathes out, all with great effort. "We'll talk about this later, yeah? I think first things first—we need to find her."

After an hour of driving in circles, June is nowhere to be seen. My mind can't help itself from circulating thoughts she might have brought herself harm.

"We'll find her," Flynn reassures me as we take another loop up the hill overlooking the village.

"What about Craig?"

Flynn looks at me sharply. "What about him?"

"Do you think she went to visit him?"

"I somehow doubt that. If she did, he'd let me know."

"You guys...talk?" I say, taking a sip of water from my bottle.

"Well, he is my dad."

"What?" I say, coughing so hard that I almost spit out all the water I had just drunk. "He's your dad?"

He shrugs indifferently, not bothered by the situation. "Biologically, yes. He was my mum's donor. They're good friends."

"Hold on," I say, trying to catalogue my thoughts into a logical sequence. Did I hear him correctly or am I still stoned from last night? "Craig, June's Craig, is your dad?"

"Why are you so shocked by this?"

"Not shocked," I say. "I'm more surprised."

"I guess after June, he knew he'd never have children, so when my mum spent several thousand quid on an anonymous donor, but it failed, he offered."

"Have you had much to do with him?"

He shrugs again. "Not really. That wasn't part of the arrangement. We've had more contact in recent years when his sister and her children moved out. I think half the town worried about him in that house, on his own and all."

As we fall into a moment of silence, I can't help but wonder who Craig is and what he's like. Then, without thinking, my curiosity gets the best of me, and I find myself pressing Flynn for answers. "What's he like?"

"Who? My dad?" Flynn laughs. "Uh...he's different. Everyone said he used to be the life of the party, but I think over time, he's pulled away from society. Loneliness, it does something to you and not always for the better."

We drive the next ten minutes in silence when I see it. June's car is parked adjacent to the break wall of the village's main beach.

"There," I yell, my panic growing when I see the driver's door wide open.

Flynn pulls in front of it, and I jump out, scanning my surroundings. The tide is in with only a short stretch of beach hugging the wall's interior.

Where is she?

I walk closer to the steps leading to the water's edge, and a flash of colour hits my peripherals. It's June sitting on a rock in the far-right corner of the bay, staring out at the open sea.

"I found her," I call back over my shoulder at Flynn before running down the stairs.

When I reach her, I know it isn't good. Her speech is unintelligible, and her lips have mottled into a dark shade of purple from the cold.

"June," I say as I struggle to keep my balance on the slick rocks. "What are you doing?"

She glances across at me, but I know she's not with me. Every time her mind shifts, it's as if it takes her soul with it, leaving only a counterfeit substitute behind.

"Hey. It's me...Abbey." I take another step towards her, careful not to frighten her. "Do you remember we came here together?"

She stares at me and abruptly stands. "Get away from me."

"June, it's me."

"Help me!" Suddenly, June screams and starts crossing the rock-strewn maze, moving closer and closer to the water's edge.

"June, please," I plead. "It's me."

I look back and see Flynn running towards us. "Abbey," he yells. "You need to get her away from the rocks. If she goes in, we won't be able to get her out."

Without thinking, I follow June and reach for her hand, which only makes her panic more.

"Help! Someone, help me!" she screams again, flailing her arms to escape my grip.

"June, please. It's me. I...I need to get you somewhere safe."

Out of nowhere, we are both hit by a wave of water, and I feel myself slipping, knocking my head as I do. As I open my eyes, I realise I'm being pummelled against the rocks by a wrath of blood-stained water.

June, where is she?

I can feel my lungs tightening, crying out for air to resurface, but I push through. Too scared if I breach the surface, any chance of finding her will be lost. I'm about to give up when I see her, floating limp in the water with her hair snaking like ropes around her shoulders. Using all my strength, I swim to her and drag her to the surface.

"Abbey," I hear Flynn call out. I blink, the salt in my eyes making it impossible to see anything but a blur.

June's heavy, heavier than I expected, and I struggle to keep us both afloat.

"Flynn," I scream. "I can't keep her up."

My mouth fills with water as we go under again. The waves are too much, and I can't stop us from crashing against the rocks a second time. When we resurface, Flynn's voice feels like it has drifted miles away.

"Abbey," he yells again. "Try to get yourself away from the rocks. I'm coming."

I hoist June up from under her arms, trying to keep her above me, but suddenly, another wave hits, and I lose grip of her as my body hits another rock, ripping the skin from my shoulder. And then, like a light switch going off, everything goes black. Completely black.

• • • •

"WHAT ABOUT THE NEXT of kin?" I hear a stranger's blurred voice ask.

"None that I'm aware of. Husband is deceased."

"Any living relatives?"

"Doesn't look like it."

"I can...help. She's my friend," I hear Flynn's voice.

I try to speak, but I can't. My arms feel heavy, as though they are encased in solid concrete, and I struggle to open my eyes, only to realise they are swollen shut.

"Her OBs are looking good. They're lucky to both make it out alive; the water must've been no more than eight degrees out there," the voice continues.

There's a gentle knock on the door.

"Doctor Eason, you're needed in room one."

"I'll be back within the hour. Just ring the bell if you need it."

As I listen, I hear the muffled shuffle of footsteps and the soft click of a door closing. Moments later, Flynn takes my hand, squeezing it gently. I want him to know I'm here, so I force myself to make a noise. It sounds like the sound of a drain gurgling more than it does human, but it's enough to let him know I'm okay.

"Abbey, you're awake."

I make the noise again, and he kisses my hand.

"I...I...thought...I thought we'd lost you," he whispers. His voice is strained as if he's carrying the weight of his guilt with every pause. "June...she's okay. A bit hypothermic and has a few bruises, but she's doing well. You...you're going to be in here a wee while." He releases my hand for a moment, and I hear him sniff. "It's my fault. I should've got to you first. I—"

I cut him off by searching for his hand and squeezing it again. Whatever he needs to say can wait. All that matters is June and I, we're both okay.

CHAPTER TWENTY-NINE

ABBEY - PRESENT

A week passes, and once the swelling in my face subsides, I'm able to visit June. Turns out, whilst June walked away with nothing more than a few scratches, I'd fractured my pelvis, and the whole right side of my body had been shattered, including my shoulder. Flynn wheels me through the corridors, and I see her. Sitting in the recreation room, she is lost in her own world, with an unfamiliar man by her side.

"Abbey," Flynn says, slowing his step as we approach the doors. "She...she doesn't remember anything. It's as if her mind has rewound itself entirely. There's no memory of coming here. There's no memory..." he pauses and looks down. I know what's coming next. It was only a matter of time, after all.

"There's no memory of me," I say gently.

Flynn starts to apologise, but I lift my one good hand to stop him.

"Hey, it's okay. I knew it would happen one day. I just didn't expect it to happen so soon."

"Are you...are you sure you're okay?"

I nod, but inside, a part of me knows I never will be. I'd prepared for it in sporadic waves, the day I became lost in the outgoing tide of memories. But it hurts, and not just at a superficial level, like a graze or the sting of a paper cut. The pain of knowing I was no longer part of June's conscious life ploughed a bed of sorrow right in the centre of my heart. It defies all sensible logic how someone I'd just met could have such a profound impact on me. Then again, maybe it wasn't so much the impact she'd had to date but more the knowing of all that could've been, which never stood a chance.

"I'm okay."

We enter the rec room, and the man glances at us. In a way, he reminds me of Flynn. They have the same piercing eyes and raven hair that is neither curly nor straight.

"Abbey," he says, bending down to extend his hand as we approach.

"I take it you're Craig?"

"Your guess would be right."

"How is she?" I ask.

He looks across at June, seated with a photo album in her lap. "Abbey, I...I think she's gone."

I feel Flynn wrap his arms around me, and my body shudders as I fight against the emotions trying to escape. "What do you mean she's gone?"

"She doesn't know any of us. For the first few days, she recognised me, but now, nothing."

"I...I don't understand."

Craig turns away from us as if trying to shield us from his pain. "The neurologist thinks she may have some form of amnesia from the fall. Either that or this is her new normal."

"Why don't we just sit for a while," Flynn interrupts. "We don't need to do this now." Before either of us can protest, he wheels me next to June, where she's focused on a photo of her and Craig. They appear to be in their early twenties seated on the bonnet of a beige Vauxhall.

I try to swallow my emotion and focus on the photo she's staring at. "I like that picture of you," I say. "Who's the handsome man?"

She smiles and her voice grows softer. "Only my greatest love."

"How did you meet him?"

She focuses on it, tracing the outline of his face with her index finger. "We met when we were kids. He came in mid-year after his parents bought a rundown farm. He was so...poor. Kids were awful to him as he always wore the same pair of holey trainers and knitted sweaters. And one day, I couldn't take it anymore and used my birthday money to buy him a new pair of shoes." She pauses, closing her eyes. "From that day on, we became two parts of one soul. It was like...we were one person."

"What happened to you two?" The sound of Flynn clearing his throat is like a warning bell, signalling his disapproval of my question, and Craig suddenly walks away.

She opens her eyes again, and confusion lines spread across her face. "I'm not sure. I think he moved away, or maybe I did."

"You never know...your paths might cross again someday."

"I hope so."

June looks at me and says, "You remind me of someone," her eyes narrowing in concentration. "I'm sorry, I didn't catch your name. What is it?"

Flynn and Craig, who by now has distanced himself, both cast their gaze to June. She's staring at me with an expression that's both satisfied and curious, like she's piecing something together in her mind.

"Abbey," I say.

"Short for Abigail?"

I laugh, wiping the tears streaming down my cheeks onto my sleeve. "No, just Abbey. What's yours?"

She ponders my question for a moment. "June."

"Like the month?"

"And the second wife of Johnny Cash."

I laugh again. "I like it."

We sit together for a while, reminiscing about her childhood memories. Though she couldn't remember Craig's face, she remembers all they did and how he made her feel. She describes her mother's garden in great detail, right down to the seasons in which every flower bloomed, but the faces of the ones she loved had been lost.

For the week while June recovers from a chest infection, we repeat the same pattern. The conversations all become a loop in a movie that'd become her life. We rehearse the lines, wear the same clothes, and bring the same food and flowers for her, never once losing hope that one day—if a miracle could be granted—it'd give her back to us just for a day. That day never comes.

"She is due to be discharged tomorrow," Craig says, taking a seat next to me. "Does she have anyone at home who can look after her?"

I shake my head, recollecting the night I met June on the bridge. "Not that I'm aware of."

After a moment of contemplation, he asks me in a tentative voice if I thought June would be willing to move in with him. It's a simple question but one that fills me with dread. I hadn't lied to just him; I'd lied to everyone, and now it was time to rip that Band-Aid off.

"I haven't been entirely honest," I say, diverting my attention to the peeling plastic armrest of my wheelchair. "When I met June, she was about to jump from an overpass into oncoming rush hour traffic. We became friends because, by her own admission, she had nobody, and I...I guess you could say I didn't want her feeling alone in the world. I'm not a friend's daughter who she considers her niece. We were complete strangers a month ago."

He studies my face for a moment as if trying to detect any trace of dishonesty in my words. "You just met a month ago?"

"Maybe more like three weeks ago."

"So, you know, right? She's left everything to you."

I open my mouth, trying to respond but the words stall. "What are you talking about?"

He reaches into his jacket and pulls out an envelope. "A week ago, I called our old lawyer's office and explained the situation, and they informed me that June had visited them wanting to change her will. She wanted to leave it all to you. The house...her savings. Everything, Abbey."

I can see the suspicion in his eyes. "I promise you, I had nothing to do with this."

"I believe you," he says, his voice lacking conviction. "Which is why, stranger or not, I want to ask for your permission. I want June to come live with me. At least, as long as she can."

I stare at him for a moment, noting the fine lines which encompass his eyes. For a man no older than June, he's aged a decade beyond his years. June had made it clear she wanted out, and if it wasn't through another attempt at suicide, she'd planned to take herself to Switzerland. Of all life had taken from her, how could I be the one to take her right to die away, too?

"Craig...I..." My words stumble as I try to force the emotions down. "June, she made it clear she didn't want to waste away. She also made it clear to me how much she loved you each and every day, even without saying it. If she had a choice, I know she'd want you to have the goodbye you deserve."

I pause again, taking a deep breath and letting it out slowly. Giving him just a week feels unkind, but if I risk giving him more time, we may lose the emotional strength to see June's final wishes through. "I'll give you a month."

He nods slowly. "And after a month? What then?"

"Then I'll take her to Switzerland."

He keeps nodding with tears streaming down his cheeks. "It's really what she wanted, isn't it?"

"It is."

"This isn't how I envisioned it." He looks longingly at the door, almost as if he's waiting for someone to come through it.

"To be honest," I say gently. "Neither did I."

It's a rare thing to see someone's heart break right in front of you. And there it was. Slowly, the more the realisation sunk in that his days with June were numbered, I watched him fall apart. It started with his breaths becoming more rapid as he tried to fight back the tears. Then he turned away, biting his right hand with his eyes closed.

I wanted to hug him and lessen the blow by assuring him everything would be okay, but even if I was physically able to, what good does lying serve? In the cruellest of contradictions, Alzheimer's had given June the courage to face something that'd haunted her for over two decades. But at the same time, it'd robbed them of the reconciliation they both deserved.

CHAPTER THIRTY

JUNE - PRESENT

It's incredible how life can change so quickly, from a clear view to a kaleidoscope of colours and confusion. I'm aware of my existence because I can feel the rise and fall as I inhale and exhale, yet my surroundings make no sense. It's as though every time I get close to understanding it, the pattern shifts.

"Are you hungry?" the man I've come to know as Craig asks.

Ignoring the soft murmurings of hunger, I shake my head.

He nods, retreating into the past and I watch as he swirls his wineglass before going on. "You've barely eaten in two days."

I apologise and blame it on the heat when in truth, I can't bring myself to eat. He never pushes it even when, in his eyes, I can see it bothers him. And it's strange because in those moments, those little moments of frustration and sadness, I don't feel confused—I feel his love.

"Let's go for a drive," he suggests, his eyes fixed on the sharp protruding angles of my wrist bones.

"Where will we go?" I ask.

"Why don't we just see where the road takes us?"

Fifteen minutes later, we are on the road with nothing but road noise filling the silence between us. The countryside rolls by like slides in a projector, and when we reach the village, Craig takes a right. We head half a mile up a narrow road before parking outside the high school. I stare at the golden plaque, straining to recall a single memory, but all that comes to me are scattered fragments.

"This is where it all started," Craig says, his eyes locked on a point in the distance.

He waits as if hoping it would spark something, and when it doesn't, his face crumples in defeat.

"I'm sorry," I say, my heart heavy with guilt. Even though he's a stranger, my intuition tells me we've crossed paths before, and I want to remember. The missing pieces are there right in front of me, and even though I can reach them, I can't breathe sense into them.

"Can I show you something?"

With a nod from me, he jumps out of the car and walks around to open my door. After helping me up, he takes my hand and leads me down a path with empty classrooms on either side. We reach a T-junction, and he stops, scanning our surroundings.

"This way," he finally says, hooking a left. The path leads us to the entrance of the hall, where he opens the door, and we step inside. As soon as I enter, the scent of polished wood and engraved bleachers fills my nostrils, evoking a wave of nostalgia.

"Wait here," Craig says as he jogs to the far end of the hall and climbs a set of stairs. As he disappears from view, the sound of "Will You Still Love Me Tomorrow" by The Shirelles fills the room and echoes off each wall, the soft melody vibrating through the floor.

I close my eyes, and slowly, the memory stutters itself alive.

In our last year of secondary school, my date was a no-show, and at the last minute, Craig borrowed one of his father's best suits and accompanied me to the debs. It hung off his yet-to-be-filled-out frame, and even though his mother safety pinned the bottoms, they dragged all over the floor. Still, he was the most attractive boy in the hall that night, saved by his effortlessly handsome looks and picture-perfect smile.

"Can I have this dance?" he said, jiving over to me playfully.

"I can't dance."

He held his hand out, a small smile playing at the corners of his lips. "You dragged me to this thing."

I covered my face, peeking through the cracks in my fingers at the bodies caught in rhythmic embraces gliding around the floor. "I'll step on your toes."

"Just one dance."

I sighed and took his hand, conceding defeat. The dancefloor was crowded, but he led me through the throngs of people, and we found a spot. Carefully, I wrapped my arms around his neck, closing my eyes as I felt the warmth of his body against mine. He smelt like Brut aftershave and peppermints, and as he pulled me closer, I felt him gently humming along to the music.

I opened one eye and glanced over his shoulder. A couple of people were smiling encouragingly, but most seemed not to know what to make of it.

From the punch table, with a smile, Nora lifted her drink in my direction.

Looking to the right of her, I saw Alice, who'd been obsessing over Craig for the past year. She kept her eyes fixed on us, and a fleeting look of disappointment crossed her face.

"Alice thinks we're an item," I whispered in his ear.

"Would it be so bad if we were?"

"Is this you asking me out, Craig McKinney?"

"That depends," he said, changing direction. "Does that mean you're saying yes?"

The sound of my name being whispered softly startles me, and I open my eyes to see the man standing before me. I study his face, noticing the same slight creases around his eyes that deepen when he smiles, and it hits me.

"Craig..." I whisper.

"Can I have this dance?" he says, extending his hand.

I take his hand, and the familiarity of our touch brings tears to my eyes. Slowly, step by step, we begin to manoeuvre around the barren dancefloor just as we had all those years ago. By the time the third song has played, I can feel myself slipping, but I fight against it, willing myself to remember.

"I'm losing it," I whisper, my grip on him becoming tighter.

With a tender kiss on my forehead, he reassures me that everything is going to be okay. "Close your eyes."

I nod and close them again, feeling the tears pooling in them break down my cheeks. It's too late. The memory is like a thin layer that is slowly being peeled away, allowing the uncertainty and fear to creep back in, and before I know it, it's gone.

The car ride back to the stranger's house is filled with an uncomfortable silence that speaks volumes about the disappointment and sadness we both feel.

We sit in silence as the car rolls to a stop in the driveway, and he looks at me with a pained expression. "I'm sorry," he whispers. "I don't know what I was thinking."

"You loved me, didn't you?" I say, noticing the tension in his jaw.

"More than you'll ever know."

"Did I love you?"

"You did." His head turns towards the window as he nods, trying to hide the tears in his eyes.

"What was our life like?"

"Our life..." He pauses and wipes his eyes, appearing hesitant to answer my question. "It was beautiful...chaotic...frustrating, but it ended too soon."

"Who ended it?"

"We both did."

I consider his words, attempting to grasp how two individuals can contribute to the downfall of a relationship when he speaks again.

"My stubbornness and pain blinded me from realising that chasing after you was exactly what you needed," he continues. "You didn't need someone to throw their hands up and admit defeat. You wanted someone to fight for you. And I...I didn't fight for you when I should've."

As if wanting to put an end to the conversation, he opens his door and jumps out. I watch as he walks up to the front door before walking back to me, looking like a man who's carrying the weight of the world on his shoulders.

"I regret it," he says, his voice barely above a whisper as he opens the passenger door. "Every day of my life, I've regretted it, and I wonder if she ever did, too."

He waits, his gaze locked on mine, waiting for me to speak, but I cannot give him the answer I know he so desperately seeks.

"I like to think she did," I say, unsure if my words will provide any solace for his grief.

Without a word, he extends his hand and helps me to stand. "I guess that's something neither of us will ever know."

CHAPTER THIRTY-ONE

ABBEY - PRESENT

Three days later, Flynn comes to visit me. When he knocks on my door, without hesitation, I welcome him in only to be greeted by someone else entirely. He'd texted me earlier that morning, telling me he had a surprise, so you can imagine my face when it wasn't just him that walked through the door first—it's Levi.

"Surprise," Levi says, waving a bouquet in his right hand. After placing them on my bedside, he draws me in for a careful hug. "You know, you could've at least texted me. I had to drive all the way here to find you."

"You drove all the way here?"

"Of course I did. The office rumour mill was saying you'd found yourself an Irishman, after all. I had to see it for myself."

I glance across at Flynn, wondering if he can see all the embarrassment I'm feeling.

"Why are you turning red?" Levi continues, and it makes me want to shove my casted fist into his mouth. "Is it him? Is he the best kiss you've ever had you texted me about?"

I'm not usually the type to blush, but my face feels like it's on fire because I realise Flynn heard everything Levi said.

"I'll leave you two to catch up," Flynn interrupts. He shoots me an amused smile, and before I can stop him, he excuses himself out the door, leaving Levi and me alone.

"Okay," Levi says, watching as the door closes. "I need all the details. Is it him?"

"No," I hiss. "He's a son of June's friend."

"And what is he to you?"

"A friend."

Levi widens his eyes. "He likes you."

"No, he doesn't."

"Yes, he does."

"He barely knows me."

"Well, he knows enough because I know that look—he's got it bad."

I stare down at my hands, remembering how yesterday, Flynn had helped me shower. My day nurse had been summoned mid-shower and told me she'd be back, but after half an hour, I was still on my own when Flynn walked into the room.

"Abbey?" he said, knocking on the door.

"I'll be out soon."

I tried to move but couldn't move within reach of the call button. After another five minutes passed, Flynn tapped on the door again.

"Is...is anyone in there with you?"

"No," I blurted out. "She said she was coming back."

"How long have you been in there?"

"Half an hour or so."

"I'm going to find someone."

Minutes after he disappeared, he reappeared with the news that they're on their way, but ten minutes later, they were still nowhere to be seen.

"I'm coming in," he said, the urgency in his voice hinting at his concern and frustration.

"No...Please, I'm okay."

"Abbey, we're both adults. I won't look, I promise."

Reluctantly, I allowed it, and Flynn entered the room to find me sitting naked with half-washed hair and my catheter bag on the floor next to me. Without hesitation, he got to work rinsing the conditioner from my hair and the soap suds from my exposed body marred with bruises.

In an effort to break the awkward silence, he joked, "Of all the times I've wanted to get you naked, Abbey, not once did I imagine this."

"I thought you weren't looking."

"It's a bit hard not to."

I was vulnerable, and not just in a physical sense. Since the accident, Flynn had broken walls in me. From talking about the death of Aila and Scott to my dreams for the future. Conversations where I once withdrew for fear of pain, I embraced because, around him, every word and syllable felt safe.

"Right," he said, turning off the water. "We better get you out of here before all your skin peels off." He walked in front of me to grab a towel, and I laughed when I saw he was soaking wet.

"I'm so sorry..." I began to apologise, but he cut me off.

"It'll dry. Did she get you a fresh gown?"

"It's on the end of my bed."

He walked out to grab it, returning seconds later. "Right, let's get you dry into this thing."

Carefully, he sponged all of the water off me. I know he's trying, but I catch him glancing at my breasts more than once as he wiped each droplet of water away. Once I'm dry, he helped me slip into my gown, and the next dilemma hit—getting me back into bed.

"I'm going to lift you," he said, his eyes trailing down at my broken limbs in cast.

"We can wait."

"You're getting cold. No, we can't. It's been nearly an hour, and we're still waiting for her to show up." He bent down to my level and studied my body as if cataloguing how best to move me since my wheelchair was nowhere to be seen. Gently, he slid one hand under my thigh, then positioned the other around my torso. "On three, ready? One, two...three."

He lifted me up so I'm against his chest, and I have my good arm wrapped around his neck.

After placing me back into my bed, he hovered for a moment with his eyes focused on my face. I wanted him to kiss me, and if reading my thoughts, he inched closer when suddenly, my door flew open, and my nurse re-entered.

"Earth to Abbey," Levi says, interrupting my thoughts.

I apologise, realising we've been sitting in silence for too long. "Sorry, I was just thinking."

"About?"

My cheeks redden further. "Never you mind."

"I drove all this way, Abbey Jane, come on now."

For once, I hoped my ability to lie would grant me an exception. Turns out today isn't going to be that day. "We kissed okay...We were both drunk, and I told him how I've never kissed, let alone slept with anyone else, and he just...kissed me."

He fights a smirk but loses the battle. "The boy has confidence."

"More like the boy has pity," I say, burrowing my face into a pillow. "I'm sure the only reason he is visiting me is because he feels guilty."

"Or maybe he likes you. Did you ever stop to think about that?"

I sigh and drop the pillow into my lap. "Even if he does, we can't do anything. My life is in London."

"A life which you hate. This could be your chance, Abbey. You could start again somewhere new."

Levi is right, and it's not as if I hadn't pondered the thought. Thing is, unlike London, where you are a nobody until you become somebody, with places like this, one minor lapse in judgement and you can't go a mile without running into it. "We're jumping the gun here. I've known the guy for two weeks."

"Stranger things have happened. When you know, you know."

"Says the guy who lectured me about being impulsive."

He laughs, casting me an amused grin. "A chance at love is the only thing worth being impulsive for."

A nurse walks in to take my OB's, and when she's finished, Levi tells me he needs to go as he'd matched with someone on a dating app who wanted to take him out to dinner.

"His username is luckoftheirish, I'm telling you now, Abbey, he better be."

"Aren't you worried about running into a closet psychopath?"

"Each and every one of us has the ability to be a psychopath. Trick is to find the ones who haven't awoken the sleeping dragon."

"That is a terrible way of thinking."

"Only a person whose celibacy is admirable would say that." He stands and gives me a soft kiss on the forehead. "You never know," he says, before making his way to the door. "We might both be blessed with some luck from the Irish."

I must have drifted off when I'm awoken by the sound of a trolley clattering from outside my door, it's dark outside. Once I've blinked myself awake, I realise Flynn must have been and gone as my customary boxed meal from the pub is on my bedside with a glass bottle of Coca-Cola.

I reach for my phone and see I've received a dozen text messages from Levi. The first, is a selfie of him waiting in the bar, followed by a series of messages about his date. From how hot he is to how his date could rival his Casey McQuiston obsession.

I text him back a reply, asking how it's going and then look at my other messages. To my surprise, there are two from Flynn.

Flynn: *Am I the best kiss you've had, or did you sneak out without telling anyone?*

And then I read the next.

Flynn*: Also, since your friend said you like to read, look inside the brown bag. Maybe this will help you understand June.*

Before I text him back, I lean forward and reach for the bag at the end of my bed. Inside, there is a box of tissues, two packets of Jaffa Cakes, and a leather-faced journal banded shut. One by one, I pull them out and place them on my lap.

Flicking the journal open to the first page, my heart suddenly drops. The journal is June's, and on the first page, in her beautifully articulate handwriting, I read the title twice: *A Million Reasons Why*

CHAPTER THIRTY-TWO

ABBEY - PRESENT

I'm torn between my desire to know what's in the journal and my guilt about invading June's privacy; nevertheless, once I start reading, I can't stop. In explicit detail, she writes about her mother's experience of early onset dementia, which started showing symptoms when she was a mere fourteen years of age. From entries about how her mother had forgotten to turn off the stove to buying the same list of groceries twice in one day. Then came the abuse.

At sixteen, June's mother had believed her to be an intruder when she arrived home late from work and had beaten her. Shortly after, June confided in a teacher about what was happening at home, and her mother was put into a psychiatric hospital. Back then, Alzheimer's wasn't fully understood and was often treated acutely as schizophrenia and other mood-related disorders. The more I read, the harder the tears fall.

By eighteen, June was already planning to end her life if she ever got the disease because, in her words, *seeing her mother change into a complete stranger broke her in ways she knew would never heal.*

I keep reading through entries where she married Craig, who gave her the most stability her life had ever seen and her efforts to reconnect with her mother. There was weeks and weeks of entries where she'd sit and read to her mother, knowing the likelihood of her remembering the visit was slim.

Then came a day I never knew existed: the day June had a termination in secret.

Desperate to know if she had the gene, she'd driven all the way to Dublin on her own to be tested. June was oblivious to her pregnancy at the time and pleaded with the doctor for a termination after a blood test confirmed that she was not only a carrier but already pregnant. At the time, it wasn't legal, so June used the only currency she could—her body—to convince the doctor to perform an illegal one.

In June's eyes, she had a million reasons to not become a parent. Each year that passed, the lies and deceit of what she'd done became more and more tangled, ensnaring her in a web that seemed impossible to escape.

Life is an intricate thing, and our experiences don't just change how we view the world, they change each tapestry which becomes our world. For all the reasons June gave for not wanting to repeat the life she'd endured, she overlooked the most important one of all. You can give a million reasons for a choice you've made, believing you know the outcome, but without doing it, there is no knowing. It's the one rule none of us can ever override, and June, she'd lived her whole life certain of something which may or may have never existed had she given it the chance.

The realisation that the night has passed and the world outside is starting to come alive hits me as I approach the final chapter. June had spent her life living in a constant state of regret, always pondering the different paths she could have taken and the choices she would have made. It'd become her biggest regret and fixation, one that changed the trajectory of her life completely.

And maybe her story isn't that far from my own. I'd been consumed by the fear of being judged and the guilt of moving on from Scott and Aila, which made me hesitant to open my heart to anyone else. Just as June had been scared of having a child for fear of repeating the experience she shared with her mother, I'd been scared that if I met someone and fell in love, it'd devalue the life I'd once shared with Scott.

"So, about last night." I hear Levi's voice and look up to see him stumbling into the room. His hair is a mess, and even from a distance, I can smell the lingering tequila and Pimm's on his breath.

"Have you even slept?" I say, checking my phone for the time. It's nearly nine in the morning.

He ignores my question and falls into the seat next to me, passing me a bagel which he's already taken two bites out of. "I could live here. Let's put it that way."

"That good, huh?"

"That good. This guy, Abbey, he's amazing."

He dives into details of the evening prior, painting a picture with his words that causes me to reconsider my cynicism towards romance. Levi's date left no stone unturned, from the mind-blowing sex to a kiss shared under the awe-inspiring sight of the Northern Lights.

"I've never had a date like it," Levi admits, unable to wipe the smile from his face.

"Well, to be honest, I doubt many people have." I pull out the bagel from its bag before passing it back to him, "You might as well finish this since you already started."

He takes it from me and doesn't hesitate to devour it within seconds. As much as I want to tell him about the journal and my plan to take June to Switzerland, I don't want to spoil the euphoric ride he's on from his date. So, in the end, I say nothing.

We fall into a brief silence when after devouring the last remaining morsel of bagel, he finally asks, "What are you going to do about Flynn?"

"Not this again," I groan.

"Do you really think this is what Scott would've wanted for you? If you push every good thing that comes your way away, a time will come when people stop trying."

He's right. I thought I knew Scott, and then after he died, I found out how little I did know. For a long time after losing him, I couldn't fathom the possibility that one day the pain would subside. But lately, the tune on that is changing. My emotional fortitude has grown stronger and deep within my soul, I can feel it charging back to life ever so slightly with each day that passes.

It seems crazy because I'm in a different country, surrounded by strangers who, a month ago, I would've passed on the street, and yet I've never felt so loved and safe. But when it comes to what Scott would've wanted for me, that's a question I've asked myself a million times and never once came within the answer's reach.

Then again, maybe it doesn't matter. All this time, I've focused on punishing myself for what happened when in reality, when we love someone, all we should care about is their happiness. If Scott loved me the way I believed he once did, he'd want me to be happy.

"Maybe I should rephrase that," Levi continues, studying my face. "Does it even matter what Scott wants? What is it you want?"

"I don't want to go back to London," I blurt out, surprised when the words leave my lips. "I mean...we both know I hate my job. I hate the city, it's just too...busy. It's always raining, and there's too many people."

Levi smiles. "Now we're getting somewhere."

"You're right; I like Flynn. I really...really like him, but if I moved here, that's a lot. We don't really know each other, and what if it doesn't work out?"

"But what if it does? You can't focus on every negative thing in life, Abbey, or you'll end up like June, who's spent her whole life in a state of what if. So, what if it doesn't work out? You come back to London, or we both pack our bags and travel the world till we find somewhere that feels like home."

"You mean that?"

"I wouldn't say it if I didn't." He pulls out his phone. "Tell me something, am I writing your resignation, or are you?"

I laugh, raising my cast arm. "If you don't mind, I'll leave that to you."

Levi heads back to his Airbnb, and I must have fallen asleep as I'm awoken by the sound of my door opening and Flynn walking in. As usual, he brought me a container of food from the pub, and as I glance at the window, I can see the sky darkening outside.

"Hey," I whisper, blinking myself awake.

"Hey," he replies. "Sorry, I'm late."

"Pub busy?"

He shakes his head without answering. I take a few mouthfuls but stop when I catch him staring at me. "Something's wrong," I say, wiping my mouth. "What is it?"

"It's nothing."

"If it was nothing, you wouldn't be looking at me like that."

For a moment, Flynn sits silent, and the seconds feel like they've turned to hours. Then he takes a seat next to me, lacing his hand into mine. "The doctors are discharging you tomorrow. They asked me if you're going back to London."

A wave of tension washes over me, causing my chest muscles to tighten and my heart to clench. "What did you say?"

"I said I'd ask you."

I clear my throat, hesitating for a moment. "Flynn..." I begin. "I don't want to go back to London. There's nothing there for me other than a job I hate which...I actually resigned from this morning. I...I, uh...I thought I'd look for a house here. I...I don't know how you feel about me." The more flustered I become, the harder it is to untangle the words in my head. "I really like you...I mean...I hate London, and I just want to have a change of pace...I like it here—"

The sound of Flynn's laughter cuts me off, and he looks down and then back to me, smiling. "Do you realise I'd made up my own speech about how I didn't want you to go back to London?"

"You did?"

"I did." He pulls my hands to his lips, kissing it gently. "Are you sure this is what you want?"

"I mean...I know what I don't want, and that's to not see how this plays out."

"Can I take you on a date then, Abbey? A proper one and all."

I laugh. "I wouldn't say no."

And for the first time in what feels like a decade, I can't help but smile.

EPILOGUE

I don't know what I expected— maybe a stereotypical white building nestled amidst the snow-capped peaks of Switzerland or a hospital of sorts. To my surprise, as Flynn and I approach the steps of a modern bungalow enveloped in stones covered in Edelweiss, I never would've guessed this to be it.

"How are you feeling?" Flynn asks, reaching for my hand.

How do you express your contentment about your best friend's imminent death without appearing insane? Truth is, I am. There's been nothing but relief since Craig finally allowed us to fulfil June's final wishes after fighting us over it for the last month. Piece by piece, June had lost all of herself, and the last week had been particularly hard. No longer able to have complete control of her bodily functions, it was the last straw.

"I'm okay," I say, glancing at the door.

The woman who opens it knows exactly who we are and who we are here to see. She smiles, pointing down the fluorescent lit hallway. "Third on the right," she says, trailing us as we follow her direction.

Her room comes into view, and I feel a lump form in my throat as I realise this is the end. When we leave here, June won't be coming home with us.

I'd mentally prepared for this moment, and now, I realise how pointless it was as the emotions override me.

"Hey," Flynn whispers, drawing me into him. "It's okay. You're alright."

It wasn't okay. How could it be? June had only lived half a lifetime; she deserved so much more. It's unjust that the world is full of evil, and yet those who perpetrate it often live long and comfortable lives, while the innocent are never given such luxury.

Once I've taken a deep breath to calm my emotions, we walk inside. The modern and well-decorated room suite does little to dispel the sense of sadness that permeates the air as June lies on her side on the queen-sized bed, centred in the middle of the room.

Flynn's gaze shifts to Craig, who sitting to the right of June, is holding her hand as if it's the only thing keeping his emotions grounded. "Why don't we leave them for a moment?"

With a reluctant nod, he stands up and follows him out of the room.

Alone, time falls into a complete stand still, and I listen in to our surroundings. There's no gentle serenading of the sea or traffic murmur. There's nothing but silence, amplifying June's deep, relaxed breaths. She wasn't afraid, and it was the one thing I'd feared she would be.

"Hey," I whisper, sitting next to her. She doesn't answer me back and instead, reaches for my hand.

"I don't know if I can do this," I say, tears cascading down my cheeks. With all the strength she can muster, she squeezes my hand again, and I look at her. Her gaze lingers on me, not with suspicion, but with a sense of familiarity. And without saying it, for the first time in months, she knows exactly where she is and who I am.

ABOUT THE AUTHOR

H. Pearce is a multi-genre author, partner, mother, and student studying mental health and creative writing. Her two areas of study often merge together in her written work, creating heart-wrenching stories that are relatable and raw. She is passionate about bringing attention to matters that are often overlooked in literature, using her areas of study to bridge the gap between what exists and real-life stories people need to read.

Printed in Great Britain
by Amazon

37824694R00128